GUN IN HIS HAND

GUN IN HIS HAND

WAYNE C. LEE

S SAGEBRUSH
Large Print Westerns

First published in Great Britain by Hales
First published in the United States by Arcadia House

Published in Large Print 2010 by ISIS Publishing Ltd.,
7 Centremead, Osney Mead, Oxford OX2 0ES
by arrangement with
Golden West Literary Agency

The moral right of the author has been asserted

British Library Cataloguing in Publication Data
Lee, Wayne C.
    Gun in his hand.
    1. Fathers and sons - - Fiction.
    2. Uncles - - Fiction.
    3. Western stories.
    4. Large type books.
    I. Title
    813.5'4–dc22

ISBN 978–0–7531–8523–0 (hb)

Printed and bound in Great Britain by
T. J. International Ltd., Padstow, Cornwall

CHAPTER
ONE

The heavy iron gates of the prison slammed shut behind Web Scott, and he followed the uniformed guard across the open space to the building that housed the warden's office.

"The warden will be mighty glad to see you," the guard said.

Scott didn't say anything. There was an oppressiveness about this place that disheartened him. It had been nine years since he had been here, and he had promised himself then that he would never come again. But that promise to himself, like so many that others had made to him, had proved to be only hollow words.

The guard opened the door into the warden's office and motioned Scott inside. The warden, a heavy-set, almost bald man, looked up from his desk.

"Webster Scott?" he asked.

Scott nodded. "They tell me you've been looking for me."

"For some time now," the warden said, coming out from behind his desk. "Your father has been asking for you."

"Why?" Scott asked bitterly. "Does he want to see for himself what a good job he has done of ruining my life?"

"It won't hurt you to see him," the warden said sharply. "He says it is very important that he talk to you now. According to him, your last visit here was nine years ago. That's a long time."

"Not long enough," Scott said.

"He's in the prison hospital," the warden said, frowning. "He'll never walk out of it. Go talk to him."

The warden nodded to the guard to open the door. Scott turned through the door, knowing the warden must think him the hardest-hearted man who ever wore boots. But the warden couldn't know all that had happened in the last ten years since Mort Scott had been sent to prison, ten years in which Web Scott had been branded the son of a jailbird everywhere he went. He might as well have rustled those cattle and pulled the trigger on Mike Hammond himself.

Scott followed the guard, barely noting his surroundings. At the far end of the big prison yard, the guard directed him into the prison hospital.

There were at least twenty men on the cots that lined either wall along the narrow room. Scott was led the entire length of the long room, while men in varying stages of illness or injury stared listlessly at him. On a cot at the far end of the room lay an emaciated man, his blue eyes blazing from sunken sockets. Scott barely recognized him.

"Web!" Mort Scott's voice was weak but filled with excitement. "I was hoping they'd find you before it was too late. Why haven't you come to see me?"

Web Scott, looking down at the shriveled, wasted form of his father, couldn't bring himself to answer.

2

Mort Scott ought to know without asking. He should have known ten years ago, when he was sentenced to life imprisonment, what life would be like for Web, the son of a jailbird.

As long as Web had stayed with his uncle, Cole Tillotson, he'd had a good job and a good place to live. But he had worn the brand of a jailbird's son, a man nobody would trust.

Then he had struck out on his own, going far away where no one knew him. He had gotten a job and had built a decent reputation. He had found a girl, the right girl for him, he had been sure. They had picked the ranch they wanted to own not far from the town where she lived and had planned to buy it. Then the roof had caved in on Scott again.

The morning that he went to the bank to get the loan to buy the ranch, word of Scott's past reached town. The son of a jailbird! The bank refused to loan him the money. The girl was shocked to find that her husband-to-be had a father in prison. She broke off the engagement and told Scott not to come to see her any more.

And then had come the call from the warden saying that Mort Scott wanted to see Web in prison. He had come, the hate in his heart so big that it crowded out everything else. If it hadn't been for Mort Scott's crime, Web would be happily married now, building up his own ranch.

"I've been mighty busy," Scott said finally.

"I've been busy, too," Mort said. "Busy dying. I had to see you, Web, before they sent me home in a box. You've been cheated."

Web frowned. Nobody needed to tell him that he had been cheated. He'd been cheated from the day he was born, having a father like Mort Scott.

"Where is Cole now?" Mort asked finally.

"I haven't seen Cole for two years," Web said. "I hear he's got a big spread over in Tomahawk Valley."

"Never heard of it," Mort said. "He cheated you, Web."

Anger surged up in Web, overriding the pity he felt for the sick man. "Cole cheated me? That's not the way I figure it. You were the one who always told me I should live without violence. Then you rustled cattle and killed the man who caught you."

Pain worked across the pinched face of the man on the cot. "Is that what you really believe?"

"What else can I believe?" Web said. "You preached no violence, yet you robbed and killed. The courts proved that. It was Cole who always told me that if I wanted to get out of life what I had coming, I'd have to take it with a gun in my hand."

"And you believed him?"

"I didn't when you were home. You know that. But after what you did, what else could I believe?"

Mort turned his face to the wall. "I should have known Cole would work on you till he changed you to his way of thinking. Why aren't you with him now?"

"I had to make it on my own. Everywhere I went with Cole, I was pointed out as the son of a jailbird. A man can't get anywhere with that brand on him."

Mort looked back at Web, the pain deeper in his eyes. "You hate me, don't you?"

4

Web shook his head. "I reckon I don't hate you. But you sure didn't leave me much room to like you, either."

"I've got to straighten you out, Web. I don't know what sickness I've got, but I'm not going to walk away from it. Take a dying man's word for it, Web. I didn't kill Mike Hammond. I didn't steal his cattle, either."

"The testimony at the trial said different."

Mort Scott nodded. "The evidence was strong, all right. But it was wrong."

"Why didn't you say so then?" Web studied Mort's face, wondering if Mort's sickness had reached his brain. Surely no innocent man would allow himself to be sentenced to prison without declaring his innocence.

"It wouldn't have helped anything," Mort said. "The evidence was all on their side. I couldn't prove anything. And if I'd tried, I would just have hurt your mother."

"How could you have hurt Mom more than you did? Letting the world believe you were a rustler and a killer hurt her more than anything."

Mort shook his head. "She never believed I did it. And nothing I could have said at the trial would have changed what the jury thought. I would only have torn down her faith in the one person she had left to depend on: her brother."

"Cole?" Web exclaimed. "Do you claim that he had something to do with that killing?"

"He had everything to do with it," Mort said positively. "But I couldn't prove it. If I'd told the court what I knew but couldn't prove, it wouldn't have

5

helped my case any, but it would have destroyed your mother's faith in her brother."

Web Scott studied the sunken cheeks and bright blue eyes of the sick man. How could he believe what Mort Scott was saying? Yet how could he doubt the truth in those eyes?

"I suppose you think Cole shot Mike Hammond," Web said.

Mort nodded. "Either Cole or that gunman friend of his, Johnny Russo. I wasn't sure at the time. But when Cole stole the Crossed S from you and sold it, it convinced me that he'd had that in mind all the time. Getting me framed for Hammond's murder was just part of the scheme."

Web leaned over the cot. "What do you mean — Cole stole the Crossed S from me? I never owned any part of that ranch. It belonged to you and Cole together."

"That's where you're wrong, Web. Cole never owned any part of it. I let him pretend to be a partner to please your mother. But he didn't own an inch of the land."

"But he claimed he owned half of it, and Mom signed over the other half just before she died."

"Did he ever make such a claim while she was living?"

Web considered, then slowly shook his head. "No, I don't think he did. What difference would that have made?"

"He wouldn't have dared say anything like that while she was living. She would have put him in his place.

The papers on the ranch were all in my name. It was to go to you, all of it."

"But Cole said Mom signed over the papers," Web objected.

"How could she sign over something she never had? Those papers were forgeries, Web. Cole stole the Crossed S from you. What did he get for it?"

"Ten thousand dollars, I heard. He never told me exactly."

"Then he owes you ten thousand dollars," Mort said with finality.

Web studied the sick man's face. There was no look of irrationality there; just the fervent desire to be believed. Could he be right?

"You still think I'm lying," Mort said when Web remained silent. "There is a little box under my cot. Look in it. You'll find a little packet of letters your mother wrote to me. You were only seventeen when she died. I'd been in here only two years. I didn't find out until a long time afterward that Cole had sold the Crossed S. I've been trying to get the warden to find you ever since. Until I was put in the hospital and the warden knew I wasn't going to get out, he wouldn't make much effort."

From under the cot, Web pulled out a little box that held the few personal belongings of his father. Digging into it, he found the package of letters neatly tied into a bundle and handed them to the sick man.

Mort tried to loosen the string holding them together, but his feeble efforts couldn't untie the knot.

"You'll have to do it," he said. "It will be the top letter, the last one she wrote me before she died. I want you to read it. You'll believe me then."

Web found the letter and took it out of its worn envelope. He recognized his mother's writing.

" 'I want to come down and see you next month,' " Web read. " 'I've been pretty poorly lately. Don't know what is wrong. But I must talk to you about signing the ranch over to Web. Cole has been trying to get me to sign the ranch over to him so that he can have a free hand in running it. He says he can make it pay off much better than it is doing now. I've told him my name isn't even on the deed, so I can't sign anything legally. But he won't listen. Since you can't be here to take care of this, I think you should sign it over to Web so that he can manage it. He is seventeen now and near enough a man to take care of it, I'm sure.' "

"Convinced?" Mort asked when Web dropped the letter in his lap.

Web nodded.

"Cole owes me ten thousand dollars," he said slowly. "But he owes you a lot more. If he did frame you for that murder, he owes you ten years of life."

"He can't repay that," Mort said wearily. "But he can pay you the ten thousand — with interest."

Web looked down at his father and saw the blaze in his eyes. "You always preached against violence."

"That was before I spent ten years of my life in this hole for something I didn't do. Any kind of violence that you use on Cole Tillotson will be too good for him!"

8

Web nodded grimly. "I'll get my ten thousand dollars from him. And I'll make him clear your name of murder and me of being the son of a jailbird. He taught me to use a gun. Maybe now he'll find out how well I learned my lessson."

"Promise you'll make Cole square things," Mort said, fighting the weariness that seemed suddenly to overwhelm him.

"I promise," Web said grimly.

He turned and started down the long aisle toward the door at the far end of the building.

CHAPTER
TWO

During the last day of riding before getting to Tomahawk Valley, Scott pushed his horse harder than usual. The time had come to face Tillotson and demand an accounting, and Scott found it hard to wait.

Scott came to Tomahawk Valley from the east. The valley was little more than a depression in the rolling plain, running northwest to southeast, a small creek cutting through its center. To the south, sand hills rolled away to the horizon, while to the north, the ground rose in long low swells, leaving no clearly marked rim to the valley.

To Scott's left was the little town. That would be Tomahawk. It didn't look like much of a place, but Scott reined that way. Information would be there, and he needed that before he faced Tillotson.

As he dropped down off the hills, his ranching eyes noticed the rich grass. This was a paradise for cattle, and there didn't seem to be enough cattle to keep the grass short. No wonder Cole Tillotson had selected this place to build his ranch.

Scott came into the town from the north and rode down the main street, noting the weathered buildings, none of which had been painted. One of the first buildings he came to housed the deputy sheriff's office, with a jail in the back. Then he rode past a block of buildings that included a hotel, saloon, hardware store and blacksmith shop. He had his eye on the livery stable down at the end of the street next to the creek. His horse had had a long trip, and Scott's first concern was for its care.

He swung down in front of the long barn, noting that the corral behind the barn enclosed a section of the creek. No watering problem for the keeper of this barn.

"Been riding quite a ways, I see," a man said, stepping out from the front of the barn.

Scott looked the man over. He was rather short and heavy-set, with piercing brown eyes that seemed to read Scott's history at one glance.

"Far enough," Scott said. "My horse needs some rest and feed."

"You've come to the right place for that," the man said. "Name's Eli Blessing."

The stable owner waited expectantly. Scott loosened the cinch on the saddle, then turned to face the man.

"Web Scott. Heard there was a man around here named Cole Tillotson. Know him?"

Blessing nodded. "Sure do. Owns the Tilted T about seven miles up the creek from here. Got business with him?"

Scott rubbed a finger along his chin. Blessing had an unhealthy curiosity, and Scott considered his answer carefully.

"I've got a deal simmering with Tillotson," he said. "I'd like to ride out there now. Got a horse I can rent? Mine is getting tired."

"He's worn to a frazzle, all right," Blessing said, looking over Scott's horse. "I've got a horse you can use. Not sure you'll find Cole at home, though."

Scott looked sharply at the stable owner. "Where do you think he is?"

"Probably out working around his cattle," Blessing said. "His spread covers a lot of territory. Just hate to see you ride out there and be disappointed."

"If he's on his ranch, I'll find him," Scott said grimly. "How about that horse?"

"I'll have to catch one from the corral," Blessing said, making no move to get the horse. "You might as well run up to the saloon and cut the dust loose while I get him."

Scott shook his head. "I'll take that horse now."

Blessing shrugged and turned toward the back of the barn. "Must be powerful urgent business."

Scott waited for the man to bring a horse, uneasiness crawling through him. Blessing seemed overly anxious for Scott to kill a little time in town before riding out to the Tilted T.

Scott tagged him as one of Tillotson's men. If so, he had probably recognized the name of Scott and right now was figuring some way to get word to Tillotson that Scott was in town looking for him.

Blessing brought a horse through the back door of the barn and tied it in a stall. Then he took his time getting a blanket and saddle on it. Scott waited impatiently. If Blessing hadn't talked to anyone outside, there was no hurry. But if he had, every wasted minute was giving a rider more of a head start so he could reach Tillotson before Scott did.

"We've got a nice valley here," Blessing said as he worked with the saddle. "Some people think Tomahawk is an odd name, though. They say Old Henry Woodruff named it. He came here long before anybody else. Found a skull with a tomahawk stuck in it about a mile from where this town stands now. So he named the valley and the creek Tomahawk."

Scott shifted his feet impatiently. "I came to see Cole Tillotson, not Henry Woodruff."

"Good thing," Blessing said. "Old Henry's dead. But he's got a boy, Josh, who owns the JW Ranch, a couple of miles west of town. You'll see it on the south side of the creek as you're going out to the Tilted T. It's a question how long Josh is going to be able to hold his ranch, though. Cole Tillotson is trying to buy him out."

Blessing backed the horse out of the stall. "Here's your horse."

Scott led the horse out of the barn into the street and mounted. Then he turned to look down at the stable owner.

"Did you send word to Tillotson that I was here?"

A flash of surprise crossed Blessing's face; then he returned Scott's stare unflinchingly. "He'll find it out soon enough."

Scott reined up the street and turned west into the road that ran along the north side of the hotel. The horse was fresh and eager to run, and Scott let him pick his own pace over the flat floor of the valley.

A couple of miles from town, Scott saw the JW Ranch on the south side of the creek, just as Blessing had said he would. It was a good-looking place, with nice buildings, well kept up.

The main road stayed on the north side of the creek, and as he rode along, Scott noticed a couple of small sets of abandoned buildings. And then ahead of him, on a knoll overlooking the creek, he spotted the white buildings of what he guessed was the Tilted T.

There was only one man in the yard when Scott rode up. He stood below the porch of the house, hands on hips, staring at Scott.

"You were expecting me, weren't you, Johnny?" Scott asked, reining to a stop.

Johnny Russo glared at Scott. "Nobody invited you."

Russo had come to the Crossed S just before Mort Scott had been arrested for murdering Mike Hammond, and he had been with Tillotson ever since. Scott knew him as rather slow-witted, but willing and able to do any job Tillotson demanded; a strong man with a very fast gun and no compunctions at all against using it in any way demanded.

"Cole at home?" Scott asked, swinging down from the saddle.

Russo shifted his big frame toward the door of the house, his smoky eyes flitting toward the house and back. "He's in there," he said.

Scott flipped the reins around the hitch rack and strode across the porch into the house. Cole Tillotson was coming from a backroom, apparently attracted by the sound of voices.

Tillotson hadn't changed much. The two years since Scott had seen him had turned his graying hair to almost snow white, which made his snapping black eyes appear brighter than ever. He still carried his six-foot frame as straight as ever, and his slimness camouflaged his almost two hundred pounds.

"I wasn't expecting to see you, Web," Tillotson said affably, pretending a surprise that Scott knew he didn't feel. "You talked like you never wanted to see me again when you cut loose a couple of years ago."

"I wanted to try my luck alone," Scott said. "I made it all right till the story of Mort's prison sentence caught up with me. I've been to see Mort. He's dying, Cole. He told me some things that I had to believe."

Tillotson turned to look out the window, and Scott guessed it was to keep Scott from seeing his face. Any doubt that Scott had been harboring concerning the truth of Mort Scott's statements vanished.

"What did he tell you?" Tillotson asked finally, turning back, his face as calm as ever.

"That you stole the Crossed S."

"And you believed him?"

"Any reason why I shouldn't?"

"You didn't believe what he said at the trial."

"You made sure I didn't," Scott said, anger slowly building up in him. "You made me believe he was a hypocrite, preaching against violence but willing to murder to get what he wanted."

"That's just how it was. The courts proved it."

"You can skip the legality, Cole," Scott said. "Mort told me what really happened and why he kept still. He couldn't prove the truth, and he didn't want to hurt my mother any more than had already been done. Also, he said the ranch was in his name only. Mom couldn't have signed over any part of it to you. So you forged that deed. I figure you owe me ten thousand dollars, Cole. When do I get paid?"

"Now hold your horses, Web," Tillotson said, his voice becoming raspy with irritation. "You'll have to prove that paper was a forgery before you've got a leg to stand on. I don't care what Mort Scott says now. That ranch was part mine, and the rest was Mort's and Lily's. When Mort went to prison for life, Lily had every right to sign over their part to me so I could make the ranch pay off."

"It paid off for you, all right," Scott said hotly. "By going back to the records, I can find out whether Mort owned the Crossed S himself or whether Mom's name was also on the deed. Mort told me you were a partner in name only. I believe that, too."

Tillotson stared at Scott for a long minute, his lips pinched together. "I'll tell you what I'll do, Web. I've felt that you should have some of the proceeds of the Crossed S Ranch, even though you aren't legally entitled to any. The ranch was mine to do with as I saw fit. Let me think about it tonight, and we'll reach some kind of settlement in the morning."

"I don't need to think about it overnight," Scott said. "You owe me ten thousand dollars. I'll settle for that and nothing less."

16

A frown tugged at Tillotson's face. "We'll talk about it in the morning. You can bed down in the bunkhouse or, if you'd rather, you can have a room here in the house."

"I'll take a room at the hotel in town," Scott said. "Have the ten thousand ready for me when I come back in the morning. With that money, maybe I can buy a ranch without having to crawl to some banker, hoping he won't turn me down because I'm the son of a jailbird. One more thing, Cole. How about telling the truth about what happened back there the day Mike Hammond was killed? Mort isn't going to get out of prison alive, anyway. But he ought to leave this world with a clean name."

Scott wheeled back through the door, leaving Tillotson scowling after him.

Scott noted again the empty houses along the road as he rode back to Tomahawk, and he wondered about them. How had Tillotson gained control of so much land in so short time? Ten thousand dollars would have bought some of it, but not nearly as much as was under the Tilted T brand now.

Scott returned the horse to the livery barn. He thought of asking Blessing about those empty houses but decided against it. Blessing's suspicious nature would do Scott no good in the long run.

He walked back up the street to the hotel and got a room. He went to sleep, wondering about his trip back to the Tilted T the next morning.

Scott wasn't sure what time it was when he was awakened by a sound in the room. It was so dark that the blackness was almost tangible. He lay still for a moment, sweeping the sleep from his mind and listening for the sound that had awakened him.

When he heard it again, it was right by his bed. He lunged to one side, but not soon enough. A heavy weight crashed down on him, almost smothering him. He lashed out with a fist and heard a grunt as he made contact with something that squashed like a pulpy nose.

A stream of soft curses poured from the man as a fist slammed into Scott's side. The man obviously wanted to subdue Scott without making enough noise to attract the attention of the other occupants of the hoel.

Scott rolled off the bed on the opposite side from his attacker. The man grunted as he lunged after him. Scott couldn't tell much about him except that he was big. Scott rolled to his knees, intent on meeting the next lunge of the man. And he'd make as much noise as he could.

But his quickly formulated plan died suddenly as he felt the cold steel of a gun nozzle pressed against his neck. He hadn't counted on two men.

"Just be quiet," the man behind the gun said. "We don't want to raise the whole town by shooting you here. But if that's the way you want it, you can have it."

Scott, on his hands and knees, remained quiet. The only sound in the room was the heavy breathing of the man sprawled across the bed.

"Now get up, and put on your pants and shirt. We're going for a walk."

"Have to have a light," Scott said.

18

"Dress in the dark or come the way you are," the man said. "Makes no difference to me."

Scott reached for the chair where he had tossed his clothes. He was sure he recognized that voice. It sounded like Johnny Russo.

He got his pants and shirt on, then pulled on his boots and moved slowly toward the door. It was so dark that he couldn't see the two men who had jumped him, but the muzzle of the gun in his back was a constant reminder of their presence.

In the hallway, there was enough light for Scott to see where he was going. He turned to look at the two men behind him and got a sharp prod in the ribs for his trouble.

"Just keep walking and go out the back door!"

Scott moved on. But he'd had his look. He had guessed right about Johnny Russo. The other man he didn't know. He was taller than Scott's six-feet-two, and bigger. Scott guessed he must weigh two hundred and forty or fifty pounds. But the thing that he'd remember best about the man was his wild blue eyes and almost bald head, although he looked to be still in his thirties.

Scott hesitated slightly before stepping into the alley behind the hotel. He could guess what was awaiting him there. But a prod from the gun drove him through the door. Fifty feet from the door, where the alley was darkest, Russo called a halt.

"Cole promised to settle with you in the morning," Russo said. "I'm going to do it now."

Scott turned to face Russo, and as he did, the big bald-headed man clubbed a fist into his side. The breath exploded from Scott, and he reeled backward. Russo moved in quickly for a man of his size and slammed his fist into Scott's face. Russo wasn't quite as tall as Scott, but he was twenty pounds heavier.

Scott lashed out in self-defense, but it was a feeble effort at best. That surprise blow in his side had taken much of the strength from him, and his fists were puny clubs against the hammering blows of the two big men.

One fist caught him at the base of the ear, and he reeled backward against a huge box that someone had dumped in the alley. Before he could move away from the box, another blow smashed into the pit of his stomach, driving out what breath he had left. Two more fists slashed at his face as he sank to the ground.

He clung to semi-consciousness and felt a sharp stab of pain as the hard toe of a boot dug into his side. The toe made two more vicious jabs before a dim voice put an end to the punishment.

"That's about enough. Cole said not to kill him this time."

A huge hand grabbed Scott's shirt front and lifted him to his feet, then held him there on sagging legs.

"Now you listen, and you listen good!" Johnny Russo hissed in Scott's face. "You get out of town just as soon as you are able. If you ever show your face in this valley again, you'll stay here, six feet under! Understand?"

Scott didn't even nod. The warning had registered, but at the moment he didn't care. Let Russo finish the job now; nobody was stopping him.

Russo let go, and Scott crumpled down against the big box. "Be gone from this country the next time I come looking for you," Russo said.

Heavy feet plodded up the alley, and Scott listened to them fade away. Then the night and the throbbing pain faded away, too, leaving peaceful oblivion.

CHAPTER
THREE

Scott wasn't sure how long he had been unconscious when he once more became aware that he was alive and hurting. It was still dark, and nothing in the alley was discernible. He pushed himself to a sitting position, gasping at the pain that shot through his head and side.

Gingerly he tested each arm and leg. No bones broken there, although his side throbbed with pain at every move. He might have a cracked rib or two, he decided.

He pulled himself to a sitting position and rested, propped against the big box. Now that he was conscious again, what could he do? He wondered if he hadn't been better off when he couldn't think.

He wouldn't find any help in the hotel. If any help had been coming from there, it would have shown up when Russo and his giant partner had come into the hotel. Instead, someone must have told them what room he was in.

The only man Scott knew in town was the livery stable owner, Eli Blessing. And Blessing would be no help. Besides, the livery stable was more than a block away. Scott didn't feel that he could drag himself that far.

After a few minutes, he got to his feet, barely able to hold back a groan as pain stabbed through his side. He stood for a minute, then began walking slowly, fighting the pain at every step.

He turned toward the hotel and within a few feet ran into a fence. Here, away from the shadow of the hotel, the thin starlight revealed a garden on the other side of the fence.

Scott moved along the fence toward the dim outline of a house. Anyone who worked in a garden should be the kind of person who would lend a helping hand to a man in need, he reasoned. And Scott was a man in need now.

It seemed like an eternity to Scott before he reached the house. It was a neat little building, painted white, and even the back yard, which Scott came through, seemed clean and free of trash.

At the back door, Scott clutched the jamb and rested before knocking. His first knock brought no response, but he hammered harder and was rewarded by a shuffle inside.

A lamp sprang to life, and a man came to the door, opening it cautiously. The man didn't say a word but, after taking one look at Scott in the feeble light of the lamp, reached out and caught Scott's arm, leading him inside.

"Mary! Ann!" he called. "I'm going to need some help."

He set the lamp on the table, then guided Scott to a couch along the wall. Running careful fingers over the bruises on Scott's face, he squinted his eyes as he examined a lump on his jaw. Then his probing fingers came down Scott's side, and Scott winced, a small cry coming from his lips.

The man nodded. "Ribs. Who did this?"

"Doesn't make any difference, does it?" Scott said. "Will I need a doc?"

Two women came through the door, each with a robe wrapped over a nightgown. The younger one came to the cot, while the older one turned to the stove and started building a fire.

"You've got a doctor whether you want one or not," the girl said.

The man spoke then. "I'm Dr. Kinkaid. This is my daughter, Anne, and my wife, Mary. Who are you?"

"My name is Web Scott." Scott looked over the Kinkaid family. He liked the honest, sincere face of the doctor. And there was genuine concern on the faces of the women.

"Somebody certainly had a mad at you," Dr. Kinkaid said.

Scott weighed his chances. He was going to need friends now more than at any time in his life. He might find them right here. But he wouldn't if he lied to them. He reasoned that his best chance was to tell the truth and hope for the best.

"I had a business deal with Cole Tillotson," he said slowly, watching their faces. "I guess this is the way he paid me off."

The doctor nodded. "That's the way, all right. Johnny Russo did this, no doubt."

24

"He and help," Scott said. "A big fellow, bald-headed."

"Dan Kale," Anne Kinkaid said quickly. "Another of Tillotson's men."

"I was out at the Tilted T this afternoon," Scott said. "I didn't see him there."

"You wouldn't," Dr. Kinkaid said. "He owns the hardware store here in town. But, like Anne says, he is one of Tillotson's men."

Scott, fighting the pain in his side, detected the bitterness in the doctor's voice. "I take it you don't cater to Tillotson yourself."

The doctor nodded. "You catch on fast enough." He unbuttoned Scott's shirt. "If you'd caught on faster, you could have avoided this."

With the hot water Mrs. Kinkaid brought from the stove, Anne gently washed the bruises on Scott's face and neck. Then the doctor bound up Scott's mid-section till he felt as if he were in a cast.

"A couple of cracked ribs there," the doctor said when he finished. "But I think much of the pain is coming from bruises. They should feel better in a few days."

Scott slid his feet to the floor and sat up, wincing at the pain. "I'm obliged to you, Doc. I'll get out of your way now."

"Where do you expect to go?" the doctor asked, staring at Scott with hands on his hips.

"Back to the hotel, I reckon. I've got a room there. I don't think I'll have company again tonight."

"You're not going anywhere," Dr. Kinkaid said flatly. "I want you right here where I can watch you for a day or two. We've got an extra room."

"Now wait a minute," Scott objected. "If Cole Tillotson wants to get rid of me bad enough to order this beating I took, he'll make it hard on anyone he finds helping me."

"I'll take my chances with Tillotson," Kinkaid said, his lips pressed tightly together. "Tomorrrow I'll pick up anything you left in your room at the hotel. Anne, will you get the spare room ready?"

"It's ready," Anne said. She took Scott's arm. "Come on now. No more objections."

If Scott had had any more objections, they faded as the appeal of a day or two of rest swept over him.

Scott hardly moved during the next day. He felt that he was one big bruise from head to foot, with a few extra bumps thrown in for good measure. Anne came into his room several times. She seemed to have taken him as her special patient.

The doctor came in just before supper time. He examined the bruises and checked the cracked ribs.

"Everything's doing fine," he said. "Now what room did you have in the hotel?"

"Room 7," Scott said. "All I left in there was my bedroll. Nothing very important in that, I guess."

"How about your horse?"

"A blaze-faced sorrel. He's down in Blessing's barn."

The doctor nodded. "Blessing will turn the horses out in the corral tonight. I can slip your horse out and bring him up here to my barn. And I'll get your bedroll from the hotel."

"What's wrong with leaving my horse down at the barn?" Scott asked, suspicion rising in him.

"I had some unusual patients at my office today," Kinkaid said. "They weren't sick; just curious. Seems they saw a horse in the corral at the barn that didn't belong there and figured his owner was still in town. If your bedroll and horse both disappear tonight, they might decide otherwise."

"You're going to do that just to hide me?" Scott asked incredulously.

"I haven't asked you anything about yourself, Scott," Kinkaid said. "But if Tillotson is enough afraid of you to have you beaten half to death to get you out of the country, you must be a real thorn in his flesh. We need more thorns for Tillotson."

"How many others hate Tillotson like you do?" Scott asked.

"Not many, I'm afraid. Josh Woodruff, maybe. But a lot of people don't like him. Ever since Tillotson came into the valley about two years ago, he's run roughshod over everybody. If he isn't stopped, the whole valley will be under his thumb in less than another year."

"I suppose you'd like to know what business I have with him?"

"I'm not asking," the doctor said. "You've got reason to fight him, and I'm hoping you'll stay and do just that."

"Cole Tillotson is my uncle by marriage," Scott said, then shook his head at the surprise on Kinkaid's face.

"Not a loving relative, as you can guess. He forged a signature and stole a ranch from me. Sold it for ten thousand dollars. I came here to collect my money. That's the reason for the beating last night I suppose he figures that pays the bill."

Kinkaid nodded. "That sounds like his way of doing things. He bought that place he built up into the Tilted T. Then he started putting pressure on every neighbor he had. Ran them out and took over their spreads. Josh Woodruff is the only other rancher left in the valley."

"Woodruff won't run?"

"He'll never run. That's why I'm afraid for him. He's about the best friend I have in the country."

"Tillotson must know you're bucking him," Scott said. "How come he hasn't run you out?"

Kinkaid looked sharply at Scott. He was a small man, only a little over five and a half feet tall and weighing about a hundred and forty pounds. But his clear blue eyes had a sharp glint in them that reminded Scott of light reflecting off steel.

"There are a couple of reasons. I'm the only doctor in Tomahawk, and even Cole Tillotson might need a doctor sometime. People here in town might not raise a fuss if another rancher was run out of the country. But it would be different if their doctor left. Tillotson would have a hornet's nest on his hands, and he knows it. I may be little, but I'll make a pretty big bump if he tries to run over me."

Scott didn't doubt that; and after listening to the doctor talk about his stand against Tillotson, he knew that he had to make a stand, too. He couldn't let this beating run him out as Tillotson hoped it would.

"You say Dan Kale is one of Tillotson's men," he said. "Is there anybody else in town that kowtows to him?"

Kinkaid nodded. "Eli Blessing down at the stable."

"I figured that," Scott said, nodding.

"And he has the deputy sheriff, Sam Hookey, in his hip pocket. The county seat is so far from Tomahawk that the sheriff doesn't get over here more than twice a year. So he put a deputy here six months ago. Tillotson somehow got his man, Hookey, into that job. So he controls what little law we have around here."

Scott shook his head. "That could make it tough."

"It is tough," Kinkaid said, "But don't you worry about it till you get on your feet again."

It seemed to Scott that that time would never come. Anne Kinkaid made sure that Scott didn't leave his room even after he was up and pacing the floor like a caged lion.

"Dad's orders," she explained. "He says that everybody is convinced that you slipped out that night he moved your horse and bedroll. He doesn't want anybody to see you until you're ready to take care of yourself."

Scott sighed. "I suppose he's right. But I can't stay cooped up here much longer. I've got a score to settle with Johnny Russo, and I won't rest easy until it's done."

"You'll have to be careful, Web," Anne warned. "Russo is a dangerous man. And what about Dan Kale? He helped Russo beat you half to death?"

"I'll think about Kale after I've taken care of Johnny," Scott said. "I've known Johnny for a long time. I figure he took a particular delight in pounding me up."

For three more days Scott roamed around the house impatiently. Then Dr. Kinkaid agreed that Scott was ready for action. After the doctor left the house for his office that morning, Scott strapped on his gun and went outside. He wasn't eager to see anyone except Johnny Russo. Here in town, only Eli Blessing at the livery stable, Dan Kale at the hardware store and possibly the desk clerk at the hotel had gotten a good enough look at him to be able to recognize him again.

He walked the streets hopefully, watching the road leading in from the Tilted T. But it wasn't until after dinner that he saw a rider come into town on that road. His pulse quickened. It was Johnny Russo, he was sure. He couldn't get close enough for a good look at the man's face before he dodged into the saloon. But he was Russo's size and had come from the direction of the Tilted T.

Checking his gun, Scott moved up the street toward the saloon. Another rider came in on the road from the west, but Scott saw that was a woman and he promptly forgot her. His business was with Johnny Russo.

Before Scott got to the saloon, however, the man he was after came out and dodged across the street toward the hotel. But instead of going into the hotel, he ducked into the alley between the hotel and Kale's hardware.

Scott speeded up. He couldn't understand Johnny Russo dodging around like that. He was obviously afraid of someone. Surely Russo couldn't know that Scott was after him. Even if he did, why would he dodge Scott like this? That wasn't like Russo.

Scott ducked down the alley between the hotel and hardware store. Behind the hardware, he got a glimpse of his man running toward the back of the barbershop.

Then things happened so suddenly that Scott dug in his heels and stopped in amazement. Two shots rang out, and the man seemed to stop in mid-stride, then stagger forward a step or two and collapse.

Following the amazement that struck Scott was a feeling of frustration. Someone had beaten him to his revenge. When nobody showed up to claim his victory, Scott ran forward. Only when he reached the fallen man did he realize that this wasn't Johnny Russo. This man was almost exactly Russo's size and had black hair like Russo, but his face was different.

Scott knelt beside hhim, as intent now on helping the man as he had been on destroying him a minute before. There was a faint pulse, but Scott saw the little seepage of blood on his chest. No man could live long with two bullets placed where these were. He lifted his eyes to trace the direction from which the shots had come and found himself looking at the back of the feed store which stood just beyond the barbershop.

Carefully Scott lifted the man and turned back toward Dr. Kinkaid's office, a ground floor room in the hotel with a side door. He winced as pain stabbed through his side. The man was as heavy as Johnny Russo, over two hundred pounds, and that was too much weight for Scott to be lifting before his ribs had completely healed.

People were coming from the street, but none offered to assist Scott in carrying the man. Dr. Kinkaid opened his office door and helped Scott get the man inside and on a couch.

"Who is he?" Scott asked.

"Josh Woodruff. I reckon Tillotson has finally killed him."

The doctor stooped to examine the wounds. After a minute he lifted his head with a sigh.

"Dead?" Scott asked.

Kinkaid nodded. "No man could live carrying two bullets where these are. Know who fired those shots?"

Scott shook his head. "I thought he was Johnny Russo, and I was trying to catch up with him to settle my score."

The doctor went through the dead man's pockets. From an inside pocket he brought out a long envelope. "It's here, all right," Kinkaid said. He looked up at Scott. "You're in for a big surprise."

"How come?" Scott asked.

But instead of answering, Kinkaid turned to the men jamming the door of the office. "Somebody bring Berwyn Edris in here."

"Who's Edris?" Scott asked.

"The only lawyer in town." He held up the envelope for Scott to see. "This is Josh's last will. He told me what's in it."

The lawyer came in a couple of minutes later, a tall, sandy-haired, blue-eyed man in his late twenties.

32

"Got a will for you to open and read," Kinkaid said, handing the envelope to the lawyer.

Edris frowned as he glanced at it. Then he turned to look at the people in the doorway. "Better make this private."

"I don't see why," Kinkaid said. "A will isn't a private affair. Let everybody know just what Josh wanted done with his property."

The lawyer's frown deepened, but he tore the envelope open. Scott watched him, wondering at his reluctance. The will was short, and Scott paid little attention to it until the last few words. "I leave to my nephew, George Ingram, one dollar. In case I meet with a violent death, I leave everything else I own, including the JW Ranch and everything in it, to the person or persons who are with me trying to help me when I die."

Dr. Kinkaid's blue eyes were twinkling as he looked at Scott. "See what I mean? You have just inherited the JW Ranch and everything on it, which must include quite a few head of cattle."

"And a barrel of trouble," Edris added, glaring at Scott.

CHAPTER
FOUR

Scott was staggered by what the lawyer had read.

"Get Hookey over here," Edris shouted to one of the men standing in the doorway.

"That deputy won't be able to find the killer," Kinkaid said disgustedly. "The only thing he can find is a bottle of whiskey and a soft bed."

"This may be different," Edris said. "He may not have to hunt far for Woodruff's killer."

Scott knew then that the lawyer suspected him of killing Woodruff. "Was Woodruff a friend of yours?" he asked.

Edris shook his head. "Not particularly. But I don't like the idea of killers running loose."

Sam Hookey came into the office two minutes later, puffing, his face red. He was a heavy man, most of his weight concentrated in the middle, where his suspenders seemed to be fighting a losing battle to hold up his pants.

"Ed said Josh Woodruff had been killed," Hookey panted.

"If you'd had your head out of that whiskey bottle, you'd have heard the shots," Edris said disgustedly. He pointed to Scott. "This stranger brought Woodruff into Doc's office."

Hookey turned to stare at Scott. "How come you got to him first?"

"I just happened to be close by," Scott said.

"Better check his gun," Edris said. "You might find Woodruff's killer without moving out of this room."

"Let's have your gun, mister," Hookey said slowly, reaching for Scott's gun.

Scott stood still while the deputy lifted the gun from its holster. Hookey broke the cylinder and squinted down the barrel. Scott watched him closely as he snapped it back in place and returned it to Scott's holster.

"Hasn't been fired since it was cleaned," he said. "He didn't have time to clean it after the shooting, did he?"

"Josh was shot only a few minutes ago," Kinkaid said. "This man had him in my office two minutes later."

"That clears him, then," Hookey said flatly. "Anybody know where the shots came from?"

"From the feed store," one man said. "I was at the blacksmith shop right across the street when it happened."

"Who did the shooting?"

"Don't know," the man said. "But I know where the shots came from, all right."

"Come on," Hookey said importantly. "Let's take a look. I'm deputizing you five men right here to go with me to look for this killer."

The deputy sheriff stamped out of the doctor's office, and the crowd followed him.

Scott turned to the lawyer. "Is that will of Woodruff's legal?"

"Of course it is," Kinkaid broke in. "Josh told me himself that he had made sure there were no loopholes in it."

The lawyer nodded slowly. "It's legal, all right. Woodruff's nephew, George Ingram, will get one dollar. Everything else goes to the man who was trying to help him when he died. I guess there is no doubt but that you're the man."

"I wasn't doing it to inherit a ranch," Scott said.

"I'm going back to my office," Edris said. "If you want to get rid of the ranch or need me for anything, you know where to find me."

After the lawyer had gone, Scott looked at Kinkaid. "Now what? I need a ranch to look after like I need a spavined horse."

Kinkaid spread a sheet over the body on the couch. "You said Tillotson stole a ranch from you. Now you have one given to you. That seems fair enough."

Scott frowned. "That's not what I came here for. I came to get the ten thousand dollars Tillotson stole from me. Woodruff's ranch isn't anything off Tillotson's nose."

"Don't be too sure about that," Kinkaid said. "Tillotson wants the JW so bad he can taste it. It's the only place in this valley that he doesn't control now. It was because of Tillotson's threats that Josh made that will."

Scott's interest quickened. "What do you know about Tillotson's threats against Woodruff?"

"I told you Josh Woodruff was a good friend of mine. He confided things to me that he wouldn't tell anyone else. He was a bachelor and he was a loner; had no close friends except me. He told me that Tillotson had threatened his life if he didn't sell to him at a dirt cheap price. Josh was stubborn as a bull. He wouldn't sell. He got the feeling some of his crew had been bribed by Tillotson. That's when he made that will."

"What good would that do?"

"Josh got suspicious of everybody. He has a foreman on the JW, Mark Sitzman, who has been with him for a good many years. Josh made a will several years ago that left the JW to Sitzman if Josh should die first. Lately Josh began getting suspicious of Sitzman, too. He made this will, leaving the ranch to the man or men who were with him at the end, fighting to help him. Josh was sure that some day Tillotson would bring his men to the JW to kill him. Josh figured that the men who stayed him in such a fight would be the loyal ones. If he got killed, he wanted them to have the ranch. If Sitzman was loyal, he'd get it. If not, he wouldn't"

"His strategy backfired," Scott said. "Sitzman wasn't in town, so he didn't have a chance to help him when he was killed."

Kinkaid nodded. "That might be. But again, maybe Sitzman wasn't with him for a reason. Josh seldom went anywhere without his foreman. But he did today. I wouldn't worry about it if I were you. I'd take the ranch."

"What about this nephew he mentioned?"

"George Ingram? I've heard Josh talk about him. Worthless as Confederate money, Josh said. He left him one dollar so he couldn't break the will, no matter how he tried."

"Just what is the JW worth?" Scott asked.

"It's a good ranch, but it has been running in trouble lately," Kinkaid said. "Josh was losing too many cattle to rustlers. I reckon Tillotson could tell something about that, too. Josh had to borrow money from me to keep going. But the ranch is worth many times what he owed."

"What about the men working on the JW? Will they stay now that Josh is dead?"

"Hard to say about that," Kinkaid said. "The men will probably stay on if they're guaranteed their pay. After all, it's still a job for them, no matter who pays their wages. But it might be a different matter with the foreman."

"Sitzman? He was a good friend of Woodruff's, wasn't he?"

"Always had been until recently, anyway. Josh was suspicious of him lately, and maybe for good reason. Mark Sitzman is no angel. He's greedy. I wouldn't put it past him to try to get rid of Josh so he could have the JW for himself."

"If that's the way it is, he isn't going to like the idea of my taking over."

"You can be sure of that. And he's got a daughter you'd better keep an eye on, too. If I was going out there, I'd watch Sadie just as close as I would Mark."

"Is she tricky?"

"Plenty," Kinkaid said. "Her mother's dead. Died before I knew them. Her father raised her like a boy, and she's as tough as any man in the country. She can outswear and outdrink any of them."

"I think I'll go out there and see what I've inherited," Scott said.

"I wouldn't go off half-cocked," Kinkaid said. "Sitzman isn't going to like the idea of you coming out to take over. I'd take the law with me, such as it is, to make him understand this is how it's going to be."

"The deputy is out looking for Woodruff's killer."

"He won't look long," Kinkaid said. "Too much work. When he comes back, make him ride out there with you. Might save an ambush."

"Think it will be that bad?" Scott asked.

"Could be. I wouldn't put much past Sitzman if he's worked up enough. And you can bet he'll be as mad as a hen in a horse tank when he finds out you own the JW instead of him."

Scott stayed close to the doctor's office until he saw the deputy come back into town with the men he had deputized. After what had happened, there was no point in keeping it a secret that he had stayed in Tomahawk. Scott was willing to bet that Cole Tillotson had long since received the information.

"Hookey's back," Scott announced to the doctor. "I think I'll go over and see him."

"Don't ask him to go out with you," Kinkaid said. "Just tell him he's going. He'll find a thousand excuses for not riding that far if you give him half a chance."

Scott left the doctor's office and walked along the side of the hotel to the street, then turned along the front of the hotel and angled across the dusty intersection to the deputy's office in the front of the jail building.

Hookey had just thrown his gun belt across his desk and dropped into his chair, his feet propped up in front of him. He scowled as he looked up at his visitor.

"What do you want?" he demanded. "I chased over half the county looking for that killer and never found a trace."

"Small county," Scott said. "You've been gone only two hours. I'm going out to my new ranch. I want you to ride out with me."

The deputy's feet thumped to the floor. "Now hold on a minute! It's noon, and I haven't had my dinner. Besides, you can find your way out to the JW without me to guide you."

"I can find my way, all right," Scott admitted. "But you're going along to convince the foreman there that I really own the ranch."

"I'm not so sure you do," Hookey growled.

"You heard what the lawyer said."

"I heard him," the deputy grumbled. "But I'm going to get a bait of grub before I go. You can like that or not."

"I can wait till after dinner," Scott agreed. "But we'll go then."

Scott went back to Kinkaid's house. He knew that Anne and Mrs. Kinkaid would have dinner for him. This would probably be the last meal he'd eat there,

40

and he was going to miss that. But it was more than just the good food that he'd miss.

"You will be careful, won't you?" Anne said as he made ready to leave after dinner.

Scott grinned easily. "I always try to finish anything I start. And I haven't got my ten thousand dollars out of Tillotson yet."

Hookey was gone when Scott got back to his office. Scott checked at the hotel, but dinner was over, and the cook there told him that Hookey had eaten and left. Remembering what Kinkaid had said about Hookey not being able to find anything but a bottle of whiskey and a soft bed, Scott headed for the saloon just across the street.

Hookey was at a table in the darkest corner, but Scott soon picked him out of the gloom. He motioned to him, and the deputy got up reluctantly and came to the door. Without a word he tramped across the side street that separated the saloon from the deputy's office and the jail.

While Hookey got his horse, Scott went back to Kinkaid's barn and got his. When he rode back to the street, Hookey was waiting, still sullen.

"No sense dragging me out to the JW," Hookey complained.

But he rode out of town with Scott. It was only two miles from town to the JW, and the two covered the distance in a short time.

The JW was a neat-appearing ranch, Scott thought as he rode into the yard with the deputy. The house was painted white, and the barn and corrals appeared in good repair. A smaller house sat behind the large one, and Scott guessed that was where Mark Sitzman and his daughter Sadie lived. There was a bunkhouse twenty yards down the slope from the big house.

"How come Woodruff had such a big house if he was a bachelor?" Scott asked.

"Josh's pappy built it," Hookey said. "The JW is the oldest spread in these parts. Old Henry Woodruff wanted an impressive mansion. In its day, that house was it."

Scott could imagine that. But he forgot the house as he saw a tall slim man with close-set eyes and thick unruly hair come from the corrals to meet them.

"Sitzman?" Scott asked softly.

Hookey nodded, then waited until the man got close. "Howdy, Mark," he said.

"What brings you out in the heat of the day, Hookey?" Sitzman demanded. "Must be something powerful important."

Hookey jerked a thumb at Scott. "He brought me. And I reckon he is a mite important. He owns the JW now."

For a long minute Sitzman simply stared, his heavy eyebrows pulled together in a dark scowl. "That's a lie!" he muttered finally. "Where's Josh?"

Scott realized that Sitzman wasn't pretending. He didn't know what had happened in town that morning.

"Ain't you heard?" Hookey asked, showing surprise himself. "Josh was killed in town this morning. Bushwhacked from the feed store. This stranger tried to help him. Carried him to the doc's office, but it was no use. Josh had a crazy will that left everything he owned to the man who was trying to help him when he died."

Sitzman started to say something, choked on the words, then tried again, "That's a lie!" he croaked finally. "If Josh is dead, I get the ranch."

Hookey leaned far over his saddle horn. "Did you know about Josh's crazy will?"

"No!" Sitzman shouted. "And I don't believe it. You'll have to show me proof."

"It's in town," Hookey said. "Edris has it. He drew up this will just a few weeks ago. And Kinkaid says Woodruff made sure there were no loopholes in it."

Sitzman looked at Scott with murder in his eyes. "He ain't going to get the JW." His hand dropped to the butt of his gun. "I'll kill him first."

"Now hold on," Hookey shouted in alarm. "Don't start any shooting, Mark. If you don't think the will is legal, check with Edris."

Sitzman glared at Scott for a moment; then his hand relaxed and came away from his gun butt. "I'll do that," he snarled. "Josh told me that this spread would be mine if anything ever happened to him. No stranger is going to walk in and take it without doing a rap for it after I've worked for Josh for ten years to get it."

A rider came charging down into the ranch yard from the west. At first, Scott thought it was one of the crew. Then he discovered that the rider was a girl. He looked at her closely. This would be Sitzman's daughter, Sadie. She could ride and swear and drink like a man, according to Kinkaid. And, looking at her in her Levi's and soiled shirt, Scott didn't doubt it. She carried a gun low on her thigh like a gunman.

"What's wrong, Pa?" she demanded.

"This jasper says he owns the JW, Sadie. Seems Josh was shot in town this morning, and he left a will, giving the ranch to whoever happened to be with him when he died. This man was there."

Sadie wheeled on Scott, her green eyes flashing fire. "You don't get this spread!" she shouted. "I don't care what any will says. You'll have to kill Pa and me to get it."

Scott jerked his head at the deputy. "Hookey here came along to see that nobody did anything foolish. Think about it, and you'll change your mind."

"My mind doesn't change that easy," Sadie said, and Scott had the feeling that Sadie's instant hatred of him would never die.

"I suppose you want us to pack up and get out," Sitzman said, his voice carrying a strong hint of the uncertainty that plagued him.

"I don't figure on making any immediate changes," Scott said. "For the time being, you can stay on as foreman if you want to."

"You're just borrowing time," Sadie observed, glaring at Scott. "The day you try to run us off the JW will be your last day on earth."

"Come on, Sadie," Sitzman said, turning toward the house behind the big white mansion. "We need to think this through."

Sadie stared at Scott for another minute before turning and leading her horse after her father.

"You'll have to watch her," Hookey warned. "She can be poison mean."

"Wonder if she ever tried being a woman," Scott said.

"She wouldn't admit it if she had," Hookey said. "Going back to town with me?"

"Why should I? This is my ranch now. I'll stay here."

Hookey shrugged. "Like you say, it's your ranch."

The deputy wheeled his horse and spurred him out of the yard as if he were glad to get away. Scott dismounted and went into the house.

He watched for the men to ride in, and when they came, he started to the corral to meet them. But the cook banged the triangle for supper, and he turned toward the cook shack and waited for the men there.

There were five men who came into the cook shack for supper. Scott introduced himself and explained what had happened. He watched their reactions. They were surprised, but there was none of the resentment that he had encountered in the Sitzmans. Though they were shocked at Josh's death, it made no difference to them for whom they worked as long as they got paid. Scott was relieved.

After supper, he returned to the big house and found a bedroom to his liking.

He was sound asleep when he heard a shot. Before his feet hit the floor, he had his gun in his hand. There were more shots, but they were some distance from the house, and Scott took time to jerk on his pants and shirt before running to the front door.

Scott guessed what it was. Tillotson had sent his Tilted T warriors to overrun the JW. Tillotson would try to wipe out all resistance to his complete control of Tomahawk Valley in one stroke.

CHAPTER
FIVE

Scott stood at the front door for a minute to get a bearing on what was happening outside. Guns were firing from the far side of the corral and were being answered to the bunkhouse. Scott saw a man dodging from the corrals to the bunkhouse, and the door of the bunkhouse swung open to let him in.

So far all the shots were being concentrated on the bunkhouse. Scott wanted to be with the men.

Splitting out the door, Scott ran toward the bunkhouse, bent low. At the door, he tapped on the panel as bullets thudded into the building around the windows through which the crew was shooting.

"Who in blazes is out there?" one man asked during a lull in the shooting.

"It's me, Scott. Let me in."

The door opened, and Scott slipped inside.

"Why did you buy into this?" one man said.

"Thought it was my fight," Scott said. "Who it is —Tilted T?"

"Who else? They figure to take over now that Josh is dead."

Scott added his gun to those already returning the fire from the corrals. "How come they didn't move in closer before starting the fireworks?"

"Good reason," one man said. "Sitzman came down after you left last night and told us to post a guard. He expected Tillotson to strike. Sam fired that first shot as a warning."

Scott frowned. Sitzman had been smarter than he had been in protecting the JW.

The shooting outside suddenly stopped. When the men in the bunkhouse stopped shooting, too, a man yelled from beyond the corrals:

"Scott, you're a dead man if you stay in Tomahawk Valley."

"How did he know you were here, Scott?" one man asked in the silence that followed.

Scott decided that somebody from town, probably Blessing or Kale, had told Tillotson that Scott had inherited the JW, and Tillotson had guessed that he would lose no time before taking over.

Suddenly a flame leaped up from a stack of hay left over from last winter. By its sudden light, Scott saw the riders heading back onto the road.

"Pulling out," one man exclaimed, emptying his gun at the riders.

"Couldn't surprise us and didn't have guts enough to fight when they found we were ready for them," another man said.

"Let's save that hay," Scott said, and broke for the door.

The men followed him as he ran toward the fire. But the dry hay was blazing fiercely, and they could do nothing to save the stack. They did manage to confine the fire to the stack and save the nearby corral fence.

Sitzman arrived at the burning stack almost as soon as the rest of the men. His close-set eyes reflected the firelight as he worked, and Scott could almost feel his rage.

"Yellow dogs!" he snapped when he stopped to catch his breath. Wouldn't stay and fight if it was an even fight. I figured they'd try to burn the house, too."

Scott knew then why Sitzman hadn't come down to the bunkhouse. He'd been back by the houses guarding them.

"Figure they'll be back?" Scott asked.

"Sure," Sitzman said. "They'll keep pecking away till they get the JW, or they're all killed. They're yellow, that's all. They've got to have every advantage or they won't fight."

With the fire out, Scott went back to the house. But he didn't sleep much the rest of the night. What would Tillotson's next move be? Scott now had something that Tillotson wanted almost as much as he wanted to get Scott out of the way. Tillotson wouldn't wait long to do something about that.

The crew stayed close to the ranch the next day. When Scott inquired about the work on the ranch, the man called Sam was quick to answer.

"Sure, there's work to be done. But Mark figures we may be needed more right here."

"Expecting Tillotson's gunmen?" Scott asked.

Sam nodded. "They tried to surprise us last night, and it didn't work. Now Mark figures they might try a raid during the daytime, figuring we'll all be out working."

Scott shook his head, remembering Cole Tillotson as he knew him. "I doubt if he'll try anything in the daylight. He might get hurt."

"He just might at that," Sam said, fondly touching the rifle beside him. "I'd like to be the one to prove that to him."

"Where's Sitzman now?" Scott asked.

"Gone somewhere. I think he's scouting the Tilted T to find out what Tillotson's got in mind."

Scott frowned. Sitzman was running the JW without any consultation with Scott. Scott didn't question the wisdom of Sitzman's moves, but he did question his motives. Was he trying to show Scott that he was boss and that Scott was just a outsider, tolerated until they could get rid of him?

Scott decided it might be wise to check the town. Tillotson had men in Tomahawk. He might learn more in town than Sitzman would at the Tilted T.

It was afternoon when Scott rode into town. Before reaching Main Street, he reined off to his right, stopping at Dr. Kinkaid's house. Anne saw him and came to the door.

"Come in, Web," she urged. "Hurry."

Scott hitched his horse and went inside. "What's the rush?"

"Don't you know you shouldn't be exposing yourself on the street like that?"

"Why not?" Scott asked. "Doesn't everybody know now that I'm a legitimate ranch owner?"

"Don't be foolish," Anne said. "You know Cole Tillotson has men in town. Dad has heard rumors.

There is a price on your head. And there are several men right here in town who would do anything for the kind of money Tillotson has put up."

"Such as Dan Kale?" Scott asked.

"He's one," Anne said. "That raid last night is surely proof enough that Tillotson will stop at nothing to get rid of you."

"I already know that," Scott said. "But how did you hear about that raid?"

"Word spreads fast in a place like Tomahawk."

"Have you any idea what Tillotson plans now?"

Anne shook her head. "We're not liable to hear any of his plans. But he's got some scheme up his sleeve, all right. Dan Kale was in Dad's office this morning, trying to find out if you really planned to stay on the JW. He dropped a hint that you'd be in for a real surprise in a day or two if you stayed on the ranch."

"That's nice," Scott said. "I like some kinds of surprises."

"You won't like this one if Tillotson has anything to do with it."

Scott felt that he was wasting time there, although talking to Anne was the most pleasant way he had ever wasted time.

"If Tomahawk is out of bounds for me, I'll head back to the JW," he said. "You can tell anybody who asks that I am staying there. I have no intention of leaving."

"I didn't think you'd run out." She followed him to the door. "Stop in whenever you can slip into town,

51

Web. If Dad finds out anything, I'll pass the information on to you."

"I'll take that as an invitation to drop in whether there is any information or not," Scott said, grinning.

Color suffused her face. "Maybe that was what it was meant to be," she said, and shut the door.

Scott didn't see Sitzman that night. The next morning, when he ran into him down by the corral, he confronted him with a question.

"Are you planning to keep the men here at the ranch today?"

"Why not?" Sitzman asked.

"Have you checked the cattle west of here since yesterday? I saw a herd being pushed across the creek by five men. Maybe they were Tilted T critters that had strayed over here, and maybe they weren't. No JW men were out there to watch."

Sitzman swore. "Why didn't you stop them?"

"I was alone. There were five of them. That herd of cattle wouldn't do me any good if I was dead."

Sitzman swore again. "I'll check the range. If Tillotson is stealing us blind, I'll put a stop to it."

"Has he been stealing JW stock?"

"We've lost some," Sitzman admitted, "but not in wholesale lots."

Scott went on to talk to the men. Anger ran through them as he told them about the cattle.

"How about letting us go out and watch today?" Sam asked. "If they got by with running off a bunch yesterday, they'll try it again today. I'd like to catch them red-handed."

The men all seemed eager, and Scott had the feeling that they agreed more with his method of handling the situation than they did with Sitzman's.

"All right; go ahead. But ride easy and stay in pairs. If some of you run into trouble, fire a couple of shots. The others will come to help."

"Come on, boys," Sam said, and wheeled toward the corral. "Make sure your shooting irons are clean and ready."

Scott turned back to see Sitzman scowling at him. "I've been foreman of the JW for ten years," Sitzman said, "and I never before had to have help giving orders to the men."

"Maybe it's time somebody did help you," Scott said, and turned toward the house. Prickles ran up his back, and he knew that Sitzman had been staring at him. But the men weren't out of sight yet. Sitzman wouldn't risk a cold-blooded murder now.

The men had been gone only a few minutes when his attention was drawn by the sound of riders approaching from the direction of town. Scott wondered for a moment if he'd been wrong in letting all the men go out on the range. Then he saw that there were only two riders. This could hardly be gun trouble coming; not from the Tilted T, anyway.

Scott stepped off the veranda of the big house to meet the two riders. One was the deputy sheriff, Sam Hookey. The other man was a stranger to Scott. He was short and not very heavy, with fiery red hair and blue eyes. His skin was pale, obviously not used to the hot sun.

"What's on your mind, Hookey?" Scott asked.

"Got somebody here who wants to meet you, Scott," the deputy said. "This is George Ingram, Josh Woodruff's nephew."

Scott studied the small man. Maybe this was the surprise that Kale had hinted was coming. It would be like Tillotson to send word to Ingram that his uncle was dead if he thought it could cause a diversion for his enemies while he plotted their final downfall. And from the looks of the anger on Ingram's face, this was going to cause a rumpus, all right.

"This was my uncle's ranch, wasn't it?" Ingram asked.

"It was," Scott said. "It's mine now."

"You're a dirty liar!" Ingram shouted, his face reddening. "I'm the only living relative of Joshua Woodruff. This ranch belongs to me."

"Not according to the will," Scott said, holding his anger in check with an effort. "And I don't take kindly to being called a liar. Didn't Hookey tell you about the will?"

"Sure," Ingram said. "Hookey told me. That law spieler, Edris, told me, too. But I don't believe a word of it. If you think you can keep this ranch from me because of a litttle scrap of paper, you can just think again. I'll take it to court, and I'll put you behind bars for stealing my property."

"You're a pretty little man to be spouting off such big threats," Scott said.

"Little, am I?" Ingram shouted. "I'll show you!"

His hand dug into his pocket, and Scott guessed he had a gun there. Scott's hand shot down and brought up his own gun. Tillotson had taught him well how to do that. The little man's hand stopped halfway into his pocket. Even Hookey stared.

"Now, now," the deputy said finally. "We'll have no guns here."

Ingram's hand came away from his pocket, and he stared for another moment at the gun that had appeared so rapidly in Scott's hand.

"Arrest him, Sheriff," he demanded.

"What for?" Hookey asked.

Scott could barely keep from smiling. Hookey wouldn't try to arrest him now even if he had a reason. He had obviously been impressed by the speed of Scott's gun hand.

"For stealing my ranch," Ingram shouted.

"According to the will I saw, he ain't stealing anything," Hookey said. "You're the one who is pushing into the wrong stall. Your uncle left you a dollar. That's all you'll get."

"I'll get more!" Ingram said. "Who's that?" He pointed to Mark Sitzman, who had just come out of his little house.

"That's Sitzman, foreman of the JW," Hookey said.

"He'll know whether there is any truth to this so-called will," Ingram said.

Ingram spurred his horse over to the JW foreman. Scott watched him as he talked to Sitzman. After a minute, he dismounted, and Sitzman invited him into the little house.

"Looks like they're going to hit it off a little better than you and him did," Hookey said.

"Looks that way," Scott agreed.

CHAPTER
SIX

Sam Hookey wasn't happy with the role he'd been handed in this affair. He hadn't wanted to make the ride out to the JW that morning. But this nephew of Josh Woodruff's, George Ingram, had come into his office right after breakfast and demanded his company.

Hookey figured there would be trouble. Ingram struck him as a trouble maker, if he'd ever seen one. So he might as well be on the spot when the trouble took place. It would save a lot of hard work investigating it all later on.

But now, as he sat on his horse and watched Ingram go into the house with Sitzman, he wondered what he should do. He might as well go on back to town. Ingram hadn't asked for an escort back to town; just out here.

Ingram didn't stay in Sitzman's house long. He came out, scowling at Scott, who had retreated to the shade of the veranda, not even inviting Hookey to get down from his horse.

"You won't stay on my ranch long, Scott," Ingram said as he swung into his saddle. "If you're smart, you'll get out now while you've still got a whole hide."

"Do you want to try to put a hole in my hide now?" Scott asked. "If you don't I'd advise you to get off my ranch and stay off."

Ingram swore loud and long as he wheeled his horse and spurred him out of the yard. Hookey had to apply his own spurs to keep up.

"Hey, hold up," he shouted when he got close enough. "You might want that horse again some day."

Ingram reined down to a trot. "I'll kill that Scott!" he snapped. "Just as sure as I'm alive, I'll kill him!"

"If you do," Hookey said, "I'll have to arrest you for murder. You sure won't kill him in a fair fight. You proved that back there a little bit ago."

"I'll kill him," Ingram repeated darkly, then rode in silence for a mile.

Hookey looked at the little man and wondered what was going on in his mind. He was tricky, Hookey decided.

"Are you in favor of Scott getting that ranch for nothing?" Ingram asked finally.

Hookey shrugged. "Can't say that I am. But there's nothing I can do about it."

"Would you do anything if you could?"

The deputy frowned. "Hadn't considered that. Don't figure the opportunity will come."

"Well, consider it," Ingram insisted. "I may need some help getting Scott off the JW. I figure you're the man to help me. That star you're wearing ought to carry a little weight."

Hookey frowned. Ingram had no idea how weightless the star really was. But maybe there was a way to use

Ingram's confidence to his advantage. He could certainly use a little boost in prestige and power in Tomahawk.

"You may be right," he said. "Got something in mind?"

"Maybe," Ingram said. "All I want to know now is whether I can depend on you for official help if I need it."

"I reckon you can count on that if you stay within the law."

Ingram was silent for another long minute. "If it wasn't exactly according to Hoyle, how would you feel? Of course, I'm not expecting your services for nothing."

Hookey grinned. Ingram was starting to speak a language he understood. "I reckon you can depend on me for any help you need, as long as we can make it look legal."

"No matter how legal or illegal it really is?"

"You said it; not me," Hookey said cautiously.

Ingram grinned. "I'll remember that. I'll let you know if you can be of help."

In Tomahawk, Ingram reined in at the livery stable, left his horse and walked up the street to the hotel. Hookey rode on to the jail and dismounted. He went into his office, mulling over the ways of twisting Ingram's presence there to his advantage.

Finally, after Ingram had disappeared inside the hotel, Hookey went back outside and mounted his horse. Cole Tillotson ought to be happy to learn what Hookey knew.

Hookey stayed on the road that clung to the north bank of the creek. After passing the JW across the creek on his left, he began thinking exactly what he would say and do when he got to the Tilted T.

A lot of men in this valley hated Tillotson. But none could possibly hate him more than Hookey did.

As he jogged along, his pace slowing as his reluctance to face Tillotson grew, Hookey thought back to the reason for his being there at all. He had made a mistake back when he was still in his teens. He had loved a girl, or thought he had.

The girl hadn't been so sure. One evening he had found her taking a boat ride with another man on the little lake close to the Ohio town where he lived. He had waited until they beached the boat, his rage growing wilder by the minute. The second the man stepped on shore, Hookey had been on him.

It hadn't been much of a fight, for the other fellow was a small man, a clerk in a store in town. After Hookey had beaten him and sent him running wildly toward town, he had turned his wrath on the girl. If she had showed fear or repentance for what she had done, his rage would have blown away. But she had been as angry as he.

His rage had exploded in his head, sending a sickening feeling washing over him. He still remembered it. He had been that angry only a few times in his life and every time it had left him sick and weak. But at that moment it had burned through him like a consuming fire.

He couldn't remember exactly what he had done. He only remembered grabbing the girl and shoving her into the water. After she was dead, he had loaded her body into the boat and rowed out to the center of the lake and shoved her overboard. Returning to town, he had spread the word that she had fallen overboard when they were out rowing and he hadn't been able to save her. He had remembered to take a dip in the lake with all his clothes on to verify his story of trying to rescue the girl.

He had thought he had covered his crime perfectly. But there had been one factor that he hadn't reckoned on. There had been a man, a bum, who had decided to spend that night sleeping in the bushes along the edge of the lake. He had heard the fight and had watched from the seclusion of his retreat. He had seen Hookey drown the girl, then take her body out into the lake and dump it.

The bum said nothing to the authorities, but had gotten in touch with Hookey a few days later and demanded enough money to make it possible for him to live at ease in society. Hookey had paid him; it had been all he could do. But it hadn't been enough. The man had come back for more money before Hookey could get it.

Hookey had left Ohio and headed west, feeling certain the former bum wouldn't follow him. But it had been a false hope. The blackmailer had found an easy living off Hookey and wasn't going to let it slip away from him.

Hookey had finally lost him in Wyoming; or at least he thought he'd lost him. He learned through an account in the paper that the man, Cole Tillotson, had just taken over a ranch down in Nebraska. Hookey at last felt that he was free of the blackmailer. But soon Tillotson had sold that ranch and moved to Tomahawk Valley. It was only a matter of weeks before Hookey had walked out into the street one day, and there was Tillotson, well dressed and prosperous-looking, but just as greedy as ever.

Tillotson had told Hookey that he needed him down at Tomahawk. At first Hookey had refused to go, but Tillotson paid no attention to Hookey's arguments. He needed him in Tomahawk. He expected him in one week; else he'd wire the authorities in Ohio what he knew about the death of that girl years ago. A week later Hookey had been in Tomahawk.

The Tilted T came in sight, and Hookey brought his thoughts back to the present. He felt like a dog crawling to the table, begging for crumbs. But if he gave Tillotson a helping hand, surely Tillotson would make life a little easier for Hookey.

Dismounting at the hitch rack, he flipped the reins over the bar and strode up the walk. He knocked and waited until Tillotson called for him to come in. It was a long wait, and Hookey did a slow burn. He had seen Tillotson's face at the window as he rode up, so he knew that the Tilted T owner was aware that he was there.

"What makes you ride out here in the sun?" Tillotson asked, scowling at the deputy.

62

"I had some information I thought you'd like to have."

After a long wait, Tillotson nodded. "Well, am I supposed to read your mind?"

"Josh Ingram's nephew is in town," Hookey said. "He's ready to do anything to get Web Scott off the JW."

"Tell me something I don't know," Tillotson said, settling back in his big chair.

"You know about Ingram?"

"I sent word to him about Josh's death," Tillotson said. "Why wouldn't I know about him?"

Hookey saw his chance for a good word from Tillotson go flying out the window. A surge of anger swept up in him, not so much at Tillotson as at the world in general. It was unfair that he always got the dirty end of the stick.

"I was trying to help you," Hookey snapped.

"Don't use that tone of voice when you're talking to me," Tillotson warned.

But the rage that had been building up in Hookey all the way out from town wouldn't be quieted that easily.

"I've got a right to use any tone of voice I choose. I am a man."

Tillotson got out of his chair. "No one would ever know it if you didn't say so."

"You've got no right to talk to me like that!" Hookey screamed.

"What rights do you think you have, anyway?" Tillotson demanded. "You ought to be rotting in a prison right now. Is that the right you're demanding?"

Mention of prison took the wildness out of Hookey's eyes, and he pinched his lips together, breathing hard.

"I tried to help you," he said finally, a whimpering note in his voice now. "I thought you'd appreciate it."

"Oh, sure, I appreciate it," Tillotson said disgustedly. "I appreciate your help like a horse appreciates a botfly buzzing around his chin."

Anger at Tillotson's unfairness swept over Hookey again. "It will be a long hot day before I ever try to help you again!"

Tillotson reached out his long arm and slapped Hookey so hard that he reeled back against the wall. "You'll do what I tell you, and you will do nothing else. Is that clear?"

Hookey thought of the gun at his hip. He knew that Tillotson carried a small derringer in a shoulder holster and could snatch it out in an instant. But still he couldn't keep his mind off that gun on his hip. If he only had that in his hand now, he'd put an end to Tillotson. He'd be a free man if Cole Tillotson were dead.

"Don't even consider it!" Tillotson snapped, stepping forward and slapping Hookey again. "I'd kill you before you had your gun out of the holster, and you know it. I don't want to kill you. I've got a job for you, and you can't do it if you're dead."

Hookey put a hand to his mouth, where blood was beginning to ooze. He considered striking back. He was almost as big as Tillotson. A good fight would make him feel better, even if he got licked. But Tillotson would never take part in a fight. He'd dodge back and use that derringer of his. Hookey was ready to face uneven odds, but not sure death.

He wheeled and ran out to his horse. Mounting, he spurred the horse viciously into a dead run out of the yard and down the road toward town. Some day he'd kill Cole Tillotson.

In Tomahawk, he left his lathered horse in front of his office, but he didn't go inside. Instead, he crossed the side street to the saloon.

"A shot of the usual?" the bartender asked when Hookey reached the bar.

Hookey shook his head. "Give me the whole bottle. A full one."

The bartender set a full bottle on the bar. "You must figure to hang on a good one."

Hookey merely grunted, went to a table along the wall and slouched down in the chair, pouring the glass brim full.

He didn't know how long he had been there when he heard the swinging doors open and looked up through bleary eyes to see Sadie Sitzman come in. The bottle in front of him was half empty. Sadie looked as if she needed company, and he had plenty of drinking whiskey. He'd show some people that he wasn't the worm Cole Tillotson thought he was. He could be somebody important, and those high and mighty know-it-alls like Tillotson could just go hang. He'd show them.

He waved a hand at Sadie. "Come over here, Sadie," he said thickly. "Drinks on me."

Sadie switched her course from the direction of the bar to Hookey's table. "Don't mind if I do, Sam. I need a drink, and I'm not particular where I get it."

"Got to be particular to drink with me," Hookey said. "Got to be somebody to be my equal."

"You're drunk already, Sam," Sadie said as she slid into the chair across the table from him.

"No, I ain't drunk. I'm just proving something."

"What?" Sadie poured some whiskey into the glass the bartender brought to her.

"That I'm just as important as anybody."

"Who says you're not?"

"A lot of people, a lot of people." Hookey wiped a hand over his face. He felt wonderful now, but it was getting hard to keep Sadie in focus over there across the table.

He poured himself another drink, spilling some of the whiskey on the table.

"You know, everybody thinks I'm just a pushover," he said, fighting to keep the words coming. "Well, I'm not. I could tell you of some of the things I've done that would prove that I'm no pushover."

"What things?" Sadie asked, leaning toward him.

Hookey grinned. Now here was somebody who was really interested in him. Sadie Sitzman was a woman after his own heart. She cared what had happened to him. She didn't think he was so unimportant.

Hookey poured his glass full again and lofted it high for a toast. He swore as some of the whiskey dribbled over the edge of the glass and down into his eyes. It stung. Just another of the unfair things that always happened to him. Well, he'd tell Sadie about the unfairness of the world toward him. She'd understand. And she'd help him do something about it, too.

He downed his drink and poured another one. While he was trying to get it to his lips, Sadie took it from his hand.

"You were going to tell me about the important things you'd done, Sam," Sadie prodded. "Don't forget."

He grinned. "I won't forget. And you won't, either, once I tell you." He wiped a hand over his face again. He had to tell her now right now, before he got to the point where he couldn't tell her anything. It was important that Sadie know of the things he had done in his life. Nothing had ever been so important before.

Later, Hookey couldn't remember just what had happened after that. He dimly remembered the bartender lifting him from the chair and half dragging him to the door. He had tried to talk to Sadie again, but he discovered that she was gone.

"It's closing time, you old fool," the bartender said.

Hookey ignored the fact that the bartender had called him a fool. Let him call him what he wanted to. Sadie could tell him that Sam Hookey was no fool; he was an important man.

When Hookey came to himself again, he was on the couch in his office. He blinked his eyes against the light and tried to sit up. His head felt as big as five heads ought to. What had happened? Had somebody hammered him on the noggin?

Then memory slowly came back to him. He had gone to the saloon last night to get drunk. He must have done a good job of it. He got to his feet and staggered over to the stove in the corner of the office. He fumbled around for a long time getting the fire started. Then he set the coffeepot on the stove and poured in water with a spoonful of freshly ground coffee beans. That hot black coffee would clear his head.

When the coffee was hot and he'd had three cups of it, his mind cleared and he began wishing it hadn't. He remembered talking to Sadie last night: But what had he told her? He couldn't remember that.

His head was feeling better and he was thinking about cooking something for breakfast when a rider pulled up at the hitch rack in front of his office. He glanced through the front window, and his insides seemed to freeze. Sadie Sitzman was dismounting.

Sadie came into the office, smiling at the rumpled appearance of the deputy. "Looks like you had a hard night, Sam," she said.

Hookey shook his head. "I'm not sure what kind of a night I had. My head is as big as a wagon box this morning."

"You really took on a jag last night, all right," Sadie said. "Feel like riding out to the JW this morning?"

"No," Hookey said. "I don't feel like doing anything but sitting right here."

"Mark wants to see you."

"Why didn't he come in?"

"He had work to do. He figured your time wasn't as valuable as his."

"You ride back and tell him it is," Hookey said.

"You'd better ride out and tell him yourself," Sadie said. "He wants to see you."

"What about?"

"He'll tell you that, too."

Hookey was feeling sick. Mark Sitzman had never had any business with him before. Now he had something urgent. What could that mean? Had Sadie told Mark something? Sitzman wasn't one to be squeamish if he saw a chance to take advantage of anybody.

"Can't it wait?" he asked.

Sadie shook her head. "Mark says to come now."

"I'll get my hat," he said. "I haven't had breakfast either."

"You took on enough liquid refreshment last night to last you till noon today," Sadie said. "Come on."

Hookey couldn't delay any longer. He got his hat and set it on his head. He scowled. The hat wasn't too tight, but it hurt this morning. His head had been aching so hard the roots of his hair were sore.

He walked down to the livery barn. Somebody had taken his horse from the hitch rack in front of his office, where he had left it yesterday, and tended to it. At the barn, he waited until Eli Blessing got the horse and saddled him. Eli was usually too slow to suit Hookey, but today it seemed he was working with the swiftness of a prairie fire.

Hookey mounted and rode out to the street where Sadie was waiting for him.

At the JW, Mark Sitzman came out and motioned for Hookey and Sadie to come on back to the little house.

"Now what is so important that I had to ride out here without my breakfast?" Hookey demanded with as much confidence as he could muster.

Sitzman led them into the house and motioned to a chair for the deputy. "Better sit down and relax, Hookey," Sitzman said. "You've had a hard night."

"What do you know about that?" Hookey asked suspiciously.

"Your tongue must be tired, too," Sitzman said. "It sure waggled a lot last night."

Hookey dropped his head and groaned. He knew what Sitzman wanted. Hookey had talked too much last night, and Sadie had passed the information on to her father. Sitzman would make use of it somehow. He was that kind of man.

"What did I say that interests you?" Hookey asked finally.

"Enough to send you to the gallows in Ohio if I wanted to tell it all," Sitzman said. "But I'm not one to talk, you know."

Hookey sat with his eyes on his boots. Evidently he had told everything. How could any man be such a complete idiot as he had been last night?

"What do you want?" he asked.

"A little legal work from you, Hookey, that's all," Sitzman said. "You can rest easy. I don't tell what I

70

know about my friends. And friends help each other out, you know."

Hookey nodded. The pattern was familiar. "What do you want me to do?"

"Just arrest Web Scott and start to jail with him. Only make sure he never gets to jail."

"Hold on," Hookey objected. "What charge will I make against Scott?"

Sitzman shrugged. "That's up to you. Surely you can think of something. It really doesn't make much difference, since he isn't going to stand trial, anyway."

"You want me to kill him?"

"I just want you to make sure he doesn't live to get to jail," Sitzman said. "Now don't tell me you can't handle a simple job like that. Any man who can deliberately drown a girl shouldn't find it too hard to shoot an unarmed prisoner. You can say the usual thing: that he tried to escape."

"I can't kill a man in cold blood."

"You can," Sitzman said. "And you'd better. It's either that or back to Ohio to stand trial for murder. Take your choice."

Hookey got up and stumbled out of the house to his office.

CHAPTER
SEVEN

Web Scott ate breakfast alone. Only the cook was in the cook shack, and he had just enough for Scott.

"Where are the rest of the men?" Scott asked.

The cook shrugged. "Mr. Sitzman said to tell you he had sent them out on the range to watch for rustlers."

Scott nodded. That sounded reasonable. After what Scott had seen a couple of days ago, it made sense to watch the herds both day and night.

Scott left the cook shack and went down to the corral for his horse. He wanted to look over the JW land a little more, anyway. He'd ride out and talk to the men. He knew that they weren't nearly so opposed to his taking over the JW as Mark Sitzman was. But he had to know whether they would fight with him or against him if it came to a showdown between him and the JW foreman.

He rode west from the house toward the spot where he had seen the cattle being pushed across the river a couple of days before. A rattlesnake, basking in the morning sunlight, buzzed as Scott's horse came too close. The horse snorted in fright and shied away. Scott quieted him, then shot the snake. He rode on. There were neither cattle nor riders on the south side of the

72

creek this morning. He circled to the south until he was sure he was at the edge of the JW land or maybe beyond. He saw little bunches of cattle here and there but no riders.

After completing a big circle that he knew must have covered most of the JW range, he headed back to the ranch. Something was funny. Where could the men be?

As he approached the ranch from the east, he saw a horse leaving the yard, coming at a hard run. He reined up and waited. But the rider didn't even see him.

It was the deputy, Sam Hookey, and Scott saw the wild look in his eyes. He seemed to be frightened half to death. Nothing else could have given him that look.

Scott, shaking his head in bewilderment, rode on down into the yard and hitched his horse to the corral bars. Mark Sitzman came out of his little house and crossed the yard to him.

"Where's the crew?" Scott demanded as soon as he faced Sitzman.

"I let them go," Sitzman said easily.

"Fired them?" Scott exclaimed. "Why?"

"We've lost a lot of cattle," Sitzman said. "We don't need so many men now."

"You fired them because you were afraid they'd take my orders instead of yours," Scott accused him.

"Prove it."

"What good would it do?" Scott said disgustedly. "I'll hire more men. And I'll make sure they take my orders."

"You won't do that while I'm here," Sitzman shouted.

"How are you going to stop me?" Scott demanded. "This is my ranch, whether you like it or not."

"It won't be for long!" Sitzman yelled.

Scott sensed that this could lead to a touchy situation. But the time for caution was past. A showdown with Sitzman had to come. It might as well be now.

He started to make a sharp retort, but the words never got past his lips. Sitzman suddenly straightened up as if somebody had clapped a hand in the middle of his back. Scott saw the surprised look flash across his face a split-second before he heard the shot. Then Sitzman sagged forward and slumped to the ground.

Scott leaned over the foreman. There was a small hole in the middle of his back where a rifle bullet had struck. Scott didn't need a doctor to tell him that Mark Sitzman had been dead before he hit the ground.

Running feet brought Scott around. Sadie was coming from the little house as hard as she could run.

"What happened?" she cried.

"Somebody shot your father," Scott said.

"Who?"

Scott looked to the east and south. The shot must have come from somewhere out there. To the south the land rose in a long swell. Not much cover for a man there. But there was a knoll to the east. A man could have hidden up there. No one was in sight now. Whoever had fired the shot had managed to vanish into the prairie.

74

"The shot came from out there somewhere," Scott said, waving a hand to the east and south.

He turned to face Sadie and saw the suspicion and hatred in her eyes.

"You did it!" she accused him.

"I did not," he denied. "He was shot in the back."

"You were the only one who could have done it," Sadie shouted, and Scott thought for a moment she was going for her gun.

The drum of a galloping horse broke the tension in the yard, and Scott turned to see the deputy, Sam Hookey, coming down the slope. He reined his horse to a sliding halt in front of Scott and Sadie.

"I heard a shot," Hookey said. "What happened?" Then his eyes fell on Mark Sitzman sprawled in the dust. "Is he dead?"

Scott nodded. "Shot in the back."

"And he killed him," Sadie said, pointing to Scott.

Scott wheeled on Sadie. "I didn't touch my gun. Anyway Sitzman was shot in the back."

"I don't doubt that," Sadie said quickly. "He might have turned his back on you. That would be the time when you'd pull your gun. You wouldn't do it when he was facing you."

Scott looked at the deputy. There was no doubting the direction of his thoughts. Sadie was convincing him. Scott appealed to Hookey, ignoring Sadie.

"You say you heard the shot, Hookey. Was it a rifle or a six-gun?"

Hookey frowned. "I can't rightly say. I was so surprised that I didn't stop to think about it."

"I heard the shot, too," Sadie said. "I was in the house. It could have been either one. Since Scott has no rifle wth him, you can be sure it was a six-gun."

"Use your head," Scott said. "I had no reason to kill Sitzman."

"I am using my head," Hookey said with conviction. "That's why I think Sadie is right. You did have a reason for killing Mark. As long as Mark stayed on the JW, you didn't have full control of the ranch. Only with him dead could you be the real boss."

"They were quarreling just before Pa was shot," Sadie said. "I heard them yelling at each other."

Hookey turned on Scott. "How about that?"

"We were quarreling, all right," Scott said. "But we were a long way from shooting it out."

"So you shot Pa before he had any idea you were planning such a thing," Sadie accused him.

Scott stared from Sadie to the deputy. There was no doubt in either of their minds now. Scott was guilty; at least they were willing to believe it.

Once an investigation was made, Scott was positive he could clear himself. For it could be proved that Sitzman had been shot with a rifle, and even Sadie would have to admit that Scott hadn't had a rifle. But before that investigation, Hookey would take him to the jail in Tomahawk. That didn't appeal to Scott. He didn't trust Hookey. He might not live to get to jail.

And even if he did, what was there to assure him that there would be an investigation of Sitzman's murder? Too many people wanted Scott out of the way. They might just accept the easy way out. They had a man arrested for the murder; they'd convict him and let it go at that. A lot of men in Tomahawk Valley would be glad to do it that way.

Scott weighed all the possibilities and always found himself on the short end of the balances. He was convicted in the eyes of Hookey and Sadie, and the country would go along with them. Behind bars, he would never change anybody's mind. His only chance was to stay out from behind those bars.

Moving swiftly, he drew his gun, while Hookey, seeing his intention, only made a pass at his gun. The deputy brought his hands forward, safely away from his holster.

"Step down off that horse, Hookey," Scott ordered.

"You'll never get away from the law, Scott," Hookey said. But he dismounted quickly.

"This will prove beyond any doubt that you're guilty," Sadie said.

"You're both sure of it now," Scott said.

"You'll never get away!" Sadie shouted. "I'll dog your trail till you're dead."

"That's your privilege," Scott said grimly. "Unsaddle your horse, Hookey."

Hookey swore loudly, but he loosened the cinch and peeled the saddle off his horse.

Scott took the guns from both Sadie and Hookey, picked the rifle out of the saddle boot on Hookey's saddle, then mounted his horse.

"I'll get you, Scott," Hookey threatened. "You know that, don't you?"

"No, I don't, Hookey. I don't figure you'll crowd me too much."

Scott rode out of the yard. Looking back, he saw that Hookey was frantically saddling his horse. Sadie had thrown herself on the ground beside her father, and he could see her shoulders shaking with sobs.

He headed straight north, splashed across the creek, crossed the trail leading to the Tilted T, and kept on going north. There were some hills and gullies there where a man and horse could disappear.

As he topped a hill, he glanced back and saw Hookey just charging into the creek. Scott had a long lead. He didn't doubt that he could stay ahead of Hookey until the deputy got tired of riding in the hot sun. It wouldn't take a lot of exertion to dull Hookey's enthusiasm for a chase such as this.

Scott spurred his horse on to the north until he was out of sight of the deputy; then he reined sharply to the west. His horse was leaving very little trace of his passing in the short buffalo grass. If Scott could keep out of the deputy's sight, he was sure he could soon lose him. He doubted if Hookey had been given the job of deputy because of his bravery or his tracking skills.

Scott followed a swale around the crest of another knoll, and there he reined up and dismounted. Moving up to a level where he could see his back trail, he watched until Hookey came in sight. The deputy went straight on north, not even bothering to study the faint tracks in the grass that might have told him that Scott had turned west.

After Hookey was out of sight, Scott mounted and rode on. Now he had to reason out who had killed Mark Sitzman and where he would be likely to find the killer.

Sitzman had been consumed with a desire to hold onto the JW for himself. Scott reasoned that this fact would have made him a prime target for Tillotson. Cole Tillotson had his eye on the JW, the only ranch in the valley still holding out against his onslaught. So Tillotson would have been most happy to see Sitzman dead; happy enough, perhaps, to hire someone to kill him.

Scott angled a little to the southwest toward the Tilted T. He might find the killer he was seeking on Tillotson's spread, but he'd have to ride carefully there. Tillotson wanted him dead, too. Sitzman surely must have been a thorn in the flesh of Tillotson. But Scott was even worse. Scott wondered if that bullet back at the JW might have been meant for him instead of Sitzman.

Coming in sight of the Tilted T, Scott reined up. Following a gully, he rode in as close to the ranch buildings as he dared. There he left his horse ground-reined and went on toward the house. The barn and corrals were to one side, while the gully ran within a few yards of the rear of the house. Crouching low, he scooted up the gully until he was even with the back door.

Looking around to make sure no one was in sight, he left the gully and sprinted to the rear of the house. He tried the back door and was pleased that it opened silently at his touch.

Inside the house, he stopped and let his eyes become accustomed to the gloom. The room he was in was a sort of anteroom leading into the kitchen. It was more of a catch-all, it seemed to Scott. There was a wash tub, two boxes partly filled with fuel for the stove, some old coats that looked as if they would never be worn again, a pair of old torn boots and some tools.

Scott stepped around a shovel to get to the door into the kitchen. The kitchen was empty, and he crossed it silently. He tried to remember how the front part of the house was arranged. He had been in it the first day he'd come to the country. But he'd been in only one room, and he recalled that only vaguely. He had been concentrating on Cole Tillotson that day, not on the house he lived in.

The house seemed as silent as a tomb. Scott crossed the kitchen and was about to go into the next room when he heard someone move there. Quickly he ducked back toward a door along one wall of the kitchen. If whoever had made that sound in the next room decided to come into the kitchen, Scott would have to be out of sight or face a greater danger than he had when Hookey was thinking of arresting him for the murder of Mark Sitzman.

The first door he opened led into a dark pantry. He thought of stepping in there and shutting the door. Unless the cook came for things to start dinner, he'd never be found. But he'd learn nothing there, either. He had to find a place where he could hear what went on in the big room of the house without being seen himself.

Moving along the wall, he tried another door. This led directly into a bedroom. He hadn't expected a bedroom to open off the kitchen, but he gave it only a passing thought as he stepped into the room, closing the door softly behind him.

As he moved along the bedroom wall, he discovered that he could hear the sound of heavy breathing on the other side of the wall.

He stepped back carefully. If he could hear breathing through the wall, there was nothing to keep the sound of his own breathing from reaching the ears of whoever was in the other room.

While backing away, Scott bumped into a chair. It overturned, hitting the floor with a crash that sounded to Scott like the tocsin of doom.

CHAPTER
EIGHT

For an instant after the chair crashed to the floor, there was a deathly silence in the house. Then a voice on the other side of the partition bellowed an order.

"Joe, get that cat out of the house! I've told you to keep him out, or I'm going to kill him!"

Scott looked around frantically for a place to hide. He lifted his gun out of the holster. Probably there weren't more than two men in the house. He might shoot his way out. But even if he did, there would surely be other men outside. Anyway, he hadn't come there to get into a battle. He had come to learn what he could without giving away his presence.

Another voice came from a far corner of the house. "The cat isn't in the house. I put him out an hour ago."

"What fell then? Made enough noise to have been the cupboard. Sounded like it was in the bedroom, though. Come and see."

"I'm coming," the other voice said disgustedly.

Scott saw no hiding place. There were only a dresser and bed in the room, in addition to the chair. He heard footsteps coming from the far side of the house and he knew he had only seconds to do something.

Quickly he set the chair upright, then dropped to the floor and wiggled under the bed. He still held his gun in his hand. He was in an awkward position if it should come to a fight. But it was the best he could do on such short notice.

"Look in the bedroom, too, Joe," the man in the big room said.

Scott was sure that was Cole Tillotson giving the orders. Joe, he guessed, worked around the house and probably did the cooking.

Scott heard the man go into the kitchen and move around; then he came into the bedroom. Scott knew that if the fellow searched the bedroom as he had the kitchen, he'd be sure to look under the bed to see if the cat was hiding there.

But the man only glanced around the room, then went back through the kitchen to the main room.

"That cat ain't in the house," he said. "I looked through, under and behind everything in the kitchen."

"What about the bedroom?" Tillotson asked.

"The door was shut between the kitchen and the bedroom. He couldn't have gone in there. That cat is outside. If you'll come out, I'll prove it."

"I'm not calling you a liar," Tillotson said sharply. "But something crashed. What was it?"

"Maybe a piece of wood in the woodbox shifted," Joe said. "You're just jumpy since Web Scott showed up."

"I reckon," Tillotson said. "I don't figure on resting easy till we get rid of him."

"Here comes that fat deputy," Joe said, disgust in his voice. "He's doing an awful lot of riding in the sun lately."

"Must be something important to bring him out here again."

Scott inched his way out from under the bed. There was no need to hide there now, and he didn't like the cramped quarters, not when there was the constant danger of having to fight his way out of the house.

Out in the main room, the thump of heavy boots told Scott that someone else had come in. When the sound stopped, Tillotson spoke sharply.

"What do you want, Sam?"

"Just thought you'd want to know that Mark Sitzman is dead."

"Sitzman?" Tillotson exclaimed. "What happened?"

Scott marked Cole Tillotson off his list of potential suspects. There had been genuine surprise in his voice.

"I was out at the JW this morning," Hookey said, "and after I started back to town, I heard a shot. I hurried back and found Sitzman dead. Web Scott was there with him. Sadie was accusing Scott of killing Mark. Scott admitted that he'd been quarreling with him. So I went along with Sadie. I'll spread the word that Scott killed Sitzman. Scott won't dare show his face in Tomahawk Valley."

"Why didn't you arrest him then and there?" Tillotson demanded. "If you'd taken him to jail, nobody would have doubted it."

"He got the drop on me," Hookey admitted. "Got clean away. He rode north and kept going. I figure he's clear out of the country now."

"You numbskull!" Tillotson shouted. "How could you let him get away when you had him dead to rights? We've got to get rid of him."

"I figure we are rid of him," Hookey said. "Running like he did, he proved positively to everybody that he's guilty. And like I said, he was going north when I left his trail. It didn't look like he intended to stop."

"He will stop," Tillotson snapped. "He'll be back. He came after me for swindling him out of the Crossed S Ranch. He won't stop till I get him or he gets me."

"If he comes back," Hookey suggested, "why don't you pay him off? It might be the safest way out for you."

"Paying him off wouldn't stop him," Tillotson said. "He is convinced that I double-crossed him. He won't be satisfied with anything but my hide. I taught him myself that you've got to have a gun in your hand to get what you want, and you never let anybody cross you and go free. I never figured on him turning on me. We've got to get rid of him, that's all."

"What if he doesn't come back?"

"You imbecile!" Tillotson shouted. "I told you he will be back. Now get out there on his trail and follow it till you get him."

"He's mighty fast with that gun of his," Hookey objected. "I saw him draw."

"If you're scared of him, maybe I should send you back to Ohio," Tillotson said. "Or maybe you'd like to argue the point with Russo."

"No, no, I'll go," Hookey said so fast the words fell over each other.

Scott heard Hookey's heavy boots thumping toward the door. Then Tillotson called, "Wait a minute," and the thumping stopped.

The next instant Scott realized his danger as he heard Tillotson moving toward the bedroom door. Evidently there was something in the bedroom that he wanted to give to Hookey. Too late, Scott thought of hiding. But he had no chance to make any move.

Tillotson shoved open the door and stared in disbelief at Scott. His hand started toward his hip where he usually had his gun. It wasn't there now. Scott snapped a shot a few inches above Tillotson's head. The Tilted T owner ducked and lunged backward, shouting for help.

But Scott was already almost to the partition door between the bedroom and the kitchen. He slammed into the door just as Joe hit it from the other side. Scott's momentum sent Joe sprawling full length backward into the kitchen. Scott leaped over him and dashed through the little anteroom into the open.

His first glance was toward the barn and corrals. No one was there. The bunkhouse was on the other side of the house. If men were there, they'd have to come around the house before they could see him.

Running in a zigzag pattern, Scott dashed for the safety of the gully a few yards from the kitchen door.

He was almost to the gully when the first shot came from the house. It missed, snapping past him to bury itself in the far bank of the gully.

Two more shots came from the house as Scott dived headlong for the rim of the gully, rolling over it to the safety of the bottom. He was on his feet in an instant, running in a low crouch toward his horse, which still stood, ground-hitched, a hundred yards away.

More shots slammed into the gully bank behind him before the men at the house discovered that he was running. Then the shots came his way, one of them spraying dirt in his face as he ran. He knew the men were coming out of the house now, trying to get their sights on him as he ran along the ravine. He considered stopping and driving them back with a few shots. But if he stopped, he'd give them the motionless target they wanted.

Reaching his horse, he wheeled and fired twice in rapid succession. The pursuit halted as the three men dived for the protection of the ravine. While they were recovering their balance to shoot again, Scott mounted and put the spurs to his horse.

A few shots followed him, but the distance was too great now for accuracy. He heard Tillotson shouting and knew he was ordering Hookey and Joe to get their horses and follow him.

Scott grinned. He had easily fooled Hookey before. He didn't anticipate any trouble losing him again. Joe might be a better tracker. But tracking over the buffalo grass slopes was going to be slow work even for the best trackers.

Once out of sight of the Tilted T, Scott turned his horse east and set his mind to trying to puzzle out the answer to Sitzman's murder. Tillotson hadn't done it and hadn't ordered it done. But he had men who would kill a man without orders if the opportunity presented itself and they knew it was a job that Tillotson wanted done. There had been no regret in Tillotson when he had learned that Sitzman was dead.

When he was halfway to town, he saw dust rising from the road to his right, coming from the direction of the Tilted T. He pulled his horse to a halt behind a knoll and watched. In a short time, he saw Hookey spurring his horse along the road to town. Apparently he had given up trying to trail Scott. But Hookey was alone. Where were Joe and Tillotson?

Scott reined off to the southeast, checking the road carefully before crossing it. He wouldn't go into town just yet. When Hookey got there, the town would be buzzing with excitement. Scott would have no chance to check the saloon to see if Russo was there. He'd wait until dark to move in.

He'd need a fairly safe place to hide until dark. The creek offered the best protection around there. Trees were scarce. There were a few around the JW and some around the Tilted T, planted there several years before by the owners. But there weren't many anywhere else. Even along the creek there was nothing bigger than water willows. But they would offer some protection for him now.

If Hookey brought a posse out after him, he wasn't likely to do much looking until he got quite a distance from town. Hookey must have left Scott's trail when that trail was still leading north away from the Tilted T.

It was already well along into the afternoon. Scott wouldn't have long to wait before the shadows began to creep down from the rims of the knolls and stretch along the swales.

After a two-hour wait, the deep shades of dusk settled over the valley. Scott mounted and moved along the creek bed, letting his horse wade in the shallow stream part of the time. As darkness grew deeper, he reined his horse up on the flat land and urged him into a trot. If Hookey had taken out a posse, the chances were that the town would be almost deserted. Probably Russo would be with the posse, too. But there were other incentives drawing Scott toward Tomahawk.

If the men of the town were gone, he would run little risk in visiting Dr. Kinkaid's place. He wanted to hear what Kinkaid had learned, for he knew that the doctor would be keeping his ears open every second.

The lights in town were burning brightly as Scott approached. He rode slowly now, keeping to the shadows. Behind a barn at the edge of town, he dismounted and left his horse. A horse was too easily seen. As he headed toward the main part of town, he realized that the men of the town were not gone. Lights blazed and noise echoed along the main street. There were more men than usual in town.

Passing Dr. Kinkaid's house, Scott was tempted to stop. But if Hookey was still in town, it might be because he expected Scott to come to Tomahawk. If so,

Hookey would not overlook the possibility that Scott probably would go to Kinkaid's as soon as he got there.

So Scott moved on along the dark street, ducking into the alley behind the hotel. The box was still in the alley where Johnny Russo and Dan Kale had given him that beating. He turned into the little runway between the hotel and the hardware store.

Dr. Kinkaid's office opened off the alley, but the office was dark now. He moved closer to the street. then stopped while he was still in the shadows. There were men in the street, and half a dozen were shuffling around on the porch of the saloon directly across from the hotel.

Hookey came out of the saloon, and Scott could see that he'd been drinking but that he wasn't drunk. He had had just enough whiskey to make him loud and boisterous. Scott realized this was no place for him. He wasn't going to get the chance to corner Russo, even if the gunman was in town. Hookey surely had spread the word that Scott had murdered Mark Sitzman. Cole Tillotson had probably given orders to get Scott at any cost. If anybody discovered him there, he'd be the target of a dozen guns.

"How many of you boys are ready to ride in my posse?" Hookey demanded, his voice a little thick.

Scott tensed as he saw Johnny Russo push open the doors of the saloon and move out onto the porch.

"Shut up, Sam," Russo said. "Do you think you can track him through the buffalo grass in the dark?"

"There's enough men here now for a posse," Hookey argued, his foggy mind obviously not quick enough to follow Russo's simple reasoning.

"You had enough this afternoon," Russo said disgustedly. "You could have followed him then."

"We only had four men," Hookey said, rubbing his head as if to clear his thoughts. "I've seen Scott in action. We need more men to take him."

"You mean you're scared to face him without an army," Russo snapped. "I'll take care of him alone if I find him."

Hookey turned away from Russo. "We'll ride out first thing in the morning, men. I want you all at my office at dawn."

"Count me in," one man said. "I could use that five hundred Tillotson is offering for Scott."

A drunken whoop came from another man. "I want my share of that. Dead or alive, he said. I reckon dead would be the safest way to bring him in."

A rider came into the north end of the street, rode past the deputy's office and reined up in front of the saloon. The men swarmed around him. Scott found it impossible to hear what the man was saying. He inched out into the street, trying to hear. He had little fear of detection. No one was looking his way, and the light from the saloon didn't reach that far. Judging from the excitement that centered around the newcomer, he must have some important news.

"How about that?" one man shouted to a friend just coming out of the saloon. "Mike here says he trailed Scott. That killer came toward town."

"Suppose he's here in town now?"

"Of course not," Russo said. "He's not brainless. Where did you lose his trail, Mike?"

The rider raised his voice so that all the men on the porch could hear. "About a mile west of town. Looked like he rode south. But it was getting too dark to see, so I came on into town. Thought it might save the posse a lot of riding in the morning."

"Sure will," Hookey said, sounding more sober now. "We'll cut his trail outside town and ride him down before he knows we're after him. Bet he went back to the JW."

A man stepped out of the hotel, apparently attracted by the commotion across the street. Scott froze as he realized that the man was close enough to see him clearly, even in the shadows. He wheeled and dived into the alley. The movement caught the man's attention, and his shout turned every head in the street toward him.

"Somebody just ran down the alley!"

"It must be Scott," one man shouted, and led the rush across the street from the saloon.

CHAPTER
NINE

Scott ran down the alley, the light from the street fading quickly into the deep gloom between the buildings. Scott's mind was racing ahead, trying to pick out a place where he could hide. He'd have no chance trying to fight that many men. Anyway, he had nothing against most of those men; he had no desire to fight them. But where was he going to hide?

At the end of the alley between the two buildings, he hesitated. Then he remembered the big box in the alley. It was empty, he was sure. But was it big enough for him to get inside?

The men chasing him would expect him either to head down the alley behind the hardware store or to go to Kinkaid's house. They'd remember that Kinkaid had helped him before.

Scott was almost against the box before he saw it. This was the darkest spot in the alley, and that was in Scott's favor. Quickly he felt over the box, trying to find the open side. Footsteps were pounding down the alley behind him now. He felt trapped, like a coyote caught in a corner of a barn.

He ran his hand around the top of the box. Behind him, he heard the men stop at the end of the hotel building.

"Hurry up with that torch," one man yelled.

"Coming," another yelled from the front of the building.

Scott saw the faint shadows as the torch came down the alley. He was thankful for the caution the men were showing. It gave him an extra few seconds to hide himself. But if he wasn't completely out of sight when that torch threw its light into the alley, his time would have run out. The thin sides of that box would be no protection from bullets.

His hand found the open side of the box, facing away from the hotel. Crouching, he squeezed inside the box. It was cramped, but he felt secure. He doubted if anybody would look there for him.

Scott couldn't see what the men were doing, but he could hear them. He recognized a few of the voices. Sam Hookey was not in charge now. Scott didn't hear his voice. He doubted if he was even in the group. There was an element of danger in the chase, and Hookey had probably decided against taking any part in it. Scott recognized Johnny Russo's voice dominating the others.

"Likely he went to Kinkaid's," Russo said. "I'll take four men, and we'll go through his house, whether Kinkaid likes it or not. The rest of you head down the alley behind the stores. Check every doorway where he could hide. See if there are any open windows where he could have crawled into a building."

"What if we don't find him?" one man asked.

"It will mean that he went on to the river, I reckon," Russo said. "He may have his horse there. But I don't figure he can make it to the river without us seeing him. Even as dark as it is, we should be able to see him if he moves away from the buildings. Let's go."

Scott held his breath as the men started moving out. If he so much as breathed loudly, the men with Russo heading toward Kinkaid's might hear him. He heard the thump of their boots as they came toward him from the corner of the hotel.

Suddenly the box rocked as one man bumped into it. Scott had to shift his weight quickly to keep the box from overturning. The man swore lustily, then hurried on after Russo and the others.

When they were gone, Scott let his breath out slowly. He had his gun in his hand. But it wouldn't have done him much good if it had come to a fight with five men.

As Russo and his men approached the back door of Kinkaid's house, the light from the stars, plus the reflection of the light from Kinkaid's window, revealed them to Scott. The open side of the box was still facing Kinkaid's house.

Russo hammered loudly, and J. R. Kinkaid came to the door. The first words exchanged by the men were too soft for Scott to hear. Then Russo's voice rose in anger.

"We're going to search your house whether you like it or not," he said. "If he's here, we aim to get him. Dead or alive, it makes no difference to us."

"He's not here!" Kinkaid shouted back. "I ought to shoot you for breaking in."

"Don't try it," Russo warned. "Get out of the way. Nobody will get hurt if you behave."

Scott saw Kinkaid step back and let Russo and the four men inside. The door stayed partly open as Kinkaid looked out into the darkness. Then he disappeared, but the sliver of light still shone through the partly open door.

Scott considered leaving the box and trying to get to his horse. But he'd have to go right past Kinkaid's house to reach the place where he had left his horse. If he tried to go around Kinkaid's to get to the horse, he'd run the risk of bumping into the other men who were searching the town for him. So he waited. The search here in town would have to be given up soon.

Then Scott noticed the light from the back door of Kinkaid's house go out. In another moment it was showing again, and he realized that someone had gone through the door. In the block of light from the door, he saw a woman's figure hurrying away from the house.

That would be Anne, he knew. But what was she doing out there?

She came on toward the hotel and passed within a few feet of the box where Scott was hiding. He crawled out of the box and called softly:

"Looking for me?"

Anne gasped, then wheeled toward him. "Yes. Where were you hiding?"

"In this box," Scott said, still crouching beside the box so he wouldn't make even the faintest silhouette. "What are you figuring on doing?"

"Hiding you where they can't find you," Anne said, coming close to the box and crouching beside him.

"What made you think you could find me when Russo and his men couldn't?"

"I didn't expect you to hide from me like you did from them," Anne said simply. "But they'll come back and search this alley again. You can't stay cramped up in that small box all night."

"Reckon you're right about that," Scott said, rubbing a leg that had already begun to cramp from his confinement. "But where can you hide me?"

"I know this town well," Anne said. "You crawl back in your box for a minute or two while I check to see where the other men are. Then I'll come back and take you to a safe place."

"Why are you doing this?" Scott asked as he squeezed into the box again. "Don't you believe that I killed Sitzman?"

"Not like they say," Anne said quickly. "You may have killed him in a fair fight. But you didn't shoot him in the back."

"I didn't kill him at all," Scott said. "Somebody with a rifle picked him off."

He heard Anne slip away. In a few minutes she came back. Scott had been watching Kinkaid's house, expecting Russo to come out. But there had been no sign of the men. They apparently were giving the house a thorough going-over.

"Come on," Anne whispered, leaning over the box. "They've already been over the lower end of town."

"Where are they looking now?" Scott asked, crawling out of the box again.

"Most of them are around the dry goods store just south of the saloon, and a couple were nosing around the harness shop south of that."

"Where are you taking me?" Scott asked as Anne led the way along the rear of the hardware store.

"To the blacksmith shop," she said. "They've already looked around it. And I happen to know that Dick Randall, the blacksmith, never locks his side door."

"Think they won't come back?"

"I doubt if they'll go over the town twice."

Scott slipped along behind Anne, both of them pressing against the buildings, where they cast no shadows in the faint light from the stars.

They crossed the open alleys between the hardware and the barbershop and the feed store, then moved along the side of the feed store until they reached the street. Scott looked at the blacksmith shop, sitting squat and dark directly across the street from them.

"I hope we can get across the street without being seen," Anne said dubiously.

"I'll go first," Scott said. "I'll walk across like I was one of the searchers. From where they are, they won't be able to tell the difference."

"Good luck," Anne said. "The door that will be unlocked is on the south side, directly across the street from the livery stable. People use it as much as they do the front door."

"Thanks for the help," Scott said, and started across the street toward the blacksmith shop, trying to act like one of the hunters instead of the hunted.

He reached the front of the shop without being challenged and moved along the side of the building. The blacksmith shop occupied the corner lot, and directly across the side street from it was the livery stable. Halfway along the side of the building, Scott found the door that Anne had told him about. He turned the knob, and it opened. He stepped inside, finding it was black as a dungeon.

He stood there in the blackness, trying to adjust his eyes, but it was too dark. Outside, he heard a man shout, and Anne called back.

The running feet sounded in the street in front of the blacksmith shop. A voice Scott didn't recognize shouted again.

"What are you doing out here, Anne? You're liable to get shot."

"You wouldn't shoot a woman, would you, Mike?" Anne said.

"Not on purpose," the man said. "But we're looking for a killer, and you can bet he'll shoot first and ask questions later. So we're not taking any chances."

"I'm glad I didn't look like your so-called killer."

"You don't know how close you came to getting shot," the man said. Then he added suspiciously, "Do you think he's down in this part of town?"

"I'm looking for him just like you are," she said. "He has probably left town. You'd have found him if he hadn't, wouldn't you?"

"We sure looked every place," the man said. "You'd better get home. The next man who sees you might not recognize you like I did."

"I'll go home right away," Anne promised.

"If you do find him, you'd better tell us," the man warned. "It will go plenty hard on your old man if we find that any of you Kinkaids has been helping him."

Scott still stood by the door, hoping to get his bearings so he could move without crashing into something. But if Randall's shop was like most blacksmith shops, there would be iron bars, plowshares, wheels, wooden handles and other pieces of wood and iron lying everywhere.

He heard nothing outside until the door behind him squeaked softly. He wheeled toward it and in the light from outside saw Anne.

"You should have gone home like that man suggested," he whispered.

"I knew you weren't familiar with the inside of this shop," she said, "and it's as black in here as the inside of a cow. I'll take you to the back where you can stay out of sight, just in case somebody looks in here again. Where is your horse?"

"Out behind that barn at the edge of town west of your place," Scott said as Anne led him by the hand to the back of the shop. His arms brushed against things on either side, but Anne guided him unerringly to the rear wall.

"They can't see you here even if they look," she said. "Now I'm going to get your horse before they find it and run it out of town. They'll think you're making a run for it and go after you, I hope."

"Don't take any more chances," Scott said.

"I'm not taking any chances," Anne told him. "They can see that I'm not you. You're a foot taller than I. If I can keep them running till morning, maybe they'll cool off enough to use some reason. Then you'll have a chance."

She was gone then, slipping away silently in the dark.

Scott crouched against the wall, grumbling to himself. He hated this sneaking and hiding. Yet that had been about all he'd done since he came to Tomahawk. He fought down the temptation to walk out there on the street and have it out with Russo and Hookey and the whole lot of them.

But what would Anne think of that? She's risked too much already to keep him safely hidden. He couldn't insult her now by throwing all that away.

Ten minutes later he heard a horse galloping down the main street outside. A moment after that yells echoed up and down the street, and then came the pounding hoofs as riders raced down the street toward the river in the direction the first horse had gone. Scott grinned in the darkness. Anne had sent the men on a wild chase, just as she had said she would.

Now was the time to get out of town, Scott decided. Right across the side street from the blacksmith shop was the livery stable. Eli Blessing had turned most of the horses out in the corral behind the barn for the night. Scott should be able to catch one. He'd have to ride bareback unless he could find a saddle. But that would be better than staying in town.

He began picking his way carefully along the aisle toward the side door. He bumped into something hanging from a rafter. It swung away from him and banged into some kind of metal. The result was a reverberating noise like the clang of a bell.

Scott stood still, wondering if the sound was really as loud as it had seemed to him. He'd been crouching there in deathly silence so long he doubted if he could judge volume. Maybe the sound hadn't carried through the walls of the shop. All the men in town might have gone off, anyway, chasing his horse that Anne had sent out of town on the run.

Then he heard running feet outside and caught a glimpse of light flashing past a crack in the wall. He sank down into a crouch again, his hand resting on an anvil in front of him.

The side door opened cautiously and a man came in, a lantern held high above his head. In his right hand, the man held a gun. Scott watched him as he carefully moved a few feet inside the door. It was Dan Kale, the hardware owner. Scott thought of the beating Kale and Russo had given him his first night in Tomahawk, and his fists balled at his sides.

Scott watched the door for more men. But none came. Maybe Kale was the only man left in town. Or maybe he had been the only one close enough to hear the clang Scott had caused.

Kale moved inside the building, looking in every direction. Scott crouched lower behind the anvil. He fingered the butt of his gun but decided against using it. He'd have the advantage, all right, if it came to guns now. But if there were other men in town, a shot would bring them on the run.

As Kale moved closer, Scott tensed, awaiting his chance. Then Kale was even with him, and as he turned his head to look in the other direction, Scott lunged at him.

Kale heard him and wheeled, bringing his gun around. But Scott hit his gun arm and sent the gun spinning. The lantern fell but somehow managed to land right side up, even the globe remaining intact.

With a wild curse, Kale lunged at Scott. But tonight Scott wasn't at the disadvantage he had been at that first night behind the hotel. He moved to one side as far as the anvil would let him and crashed a fist into Kale's face. Blood spurted, and Kale cursed loudly. He wheeled back, and again Scott weaved away from his wild swings, landing telling blows of his own.

Kale turned back again, determined to get his hands on Scott. Big as the man was, Scott didn't doubt that Kale could crush him if he got him in those big arms. Kale threw himself at Scott, arms wide to keep Scott from escaping again. But Scott ducked low and scooted away. Kale, unable to halt his lunge, hit the anvil, one knee crashing against the solid iron.

With a cry of pain, he turned back toward Scott, barely able to stand. But still he came on. Scott moved in to meet him and hammered his face with hard blows. Kale retreated until he backed into the forge and plopped down in the ashes. They were still hot from the day's work, and Kale rolled away, yelling and cursing.

He got to his knees and dived forward at Scott. Scott had to admire his courage but not his good sense. The man had no idea when to quit. Scott hammered a fist down on the back of Kale's neck with all his force, and Kale sprawled out like a dead man.

Scott turned toward the door just as Anne came running in, breathless. She took in the scene at one glance. The lantern still sat where it had fallen, throwing a weird light over the interior of the shop.

"Come on, Web," Anne said quickly. "Others heard the fight, too. You'll have to run for it."

"Where to?" Scott asked as he ran to the door.

"To our house now. They've searched it. They surely won't look there again."

Outside the blacksmith shop, Anne turned toward the rear of the building, Scott just a step behind her. They had barely turned the corner when Scott heard men pounding on the front door. Then someone came around the corner and ran for the side door.

Silently Scott and Anne ran along the rear of the buildings until they reached the side street that separated the saloon and the deputy's office. There was no sign of life at either place, and Anne led the way into the street and turned down it toward the hotel. No challenge stopped them, and they were soon at the back door of Kinkaid's place.

Anne quickly explained what she had seen in the blacksmith shop and Dr. Kinkaid grinned happily.

"I wish I could have seen Dan Kale pounded into the dirt," he said.

"You'll likely see him tomorrow," Scott predicted. "He banged a knee into the anvil pretty hard. He'll probably need doctoring."

"I may finish breaking it if it isn't already done," Kinkaid threatened.

But Scott knew that the doctor would do what he could for Kale if the man came to him.

A knock sounded at the front door and, without waiting for anyone to answer the knock Berwyn Edris came in. Scott had ducked toward his old room the instant he heard the knock. But he doubted if he had made it in time to avoid being seen by the lawyer.

However, if Edris had seen Scott, he gave no hint of it. He talked about the excitement in town and of the sounds of battle that had come from the blacksmith shop.

"I came over to see if you were all right, Anne," he said. "Mike told me how close he came to shooting you out there in the street tonight. I wish you wouldn't go out at times like this. When they said there was trouble down at the blacksmith shop, I was afraid you might be involved again. So I came over to see."

"I'm all right," Anne said sharply. "You needn't worry about me."

"I do, anyway," Edris said tenderly. "I wish you would stay inside till this trouble is over."

Scott couldn't see the lawyer, but he had the feeling that Edris' sharp eyes were searching the house. He wanted to know why Anne had been on the street tonight. That would make him doubly dangerous to Scott. For Edris made no pretense about his feelings for Anne. And Anne certainly had made no pretense tonight about her concern for Scott.

If, when he came in, Berwyn Edris caught a glimpse of Scott ducking into the room, Scott was willing to bet that the men who had gone after his horse a while ago would hear about it the moment they returned to town.

CHAPTER
TEN

Scott stayed in his room, debating whether or not he should step out and confront Berwyn Edris. The more he thought about it, the more certain he was that the lawyer had spotted him or was convinced that he was in the house.

Still, Edris was making no hostile moves. It wasn't Scott's place to cause Kinkaid any more trouble by facing Edris with a gun. So he sat quietly in his room and waited until the lawyer had left.

When he came out of the room, Anne voiced the question that had been plaguing him.

"Did he see you, Web?"

Scott shrugged. "I don't know. I wasn't expecting him to come in without an invitation, so I wasn't out of sight yet. I saw him well enough to recognize him. It's possible that he recognized me, too."

"I think he did," Anne said. "He looked right at that door a dozen times. But he didn't say a word about it."

"I'd better get out of here now," Scott said. "If I stay, it will bring more trouble down on you."

Kinkaid waved a hand. "Never mind that. Edris might not tell what he saw. He doesn't like Hookey, you know."

"How does he feel about Tillotson?" Scott asked. "He's the one who's offering the money for my hide."

Kinkaid nodded. "This is first time since Cole Tillotson came to this country that anybody has given him any real trouble. You've really put a burr under his saddle."

"I'm in no position to make it stick, though," Scott said. "Sooner or later I'm going to run out of luck. And once they get their hands on me, I won't last long. Not with that murder charge hanging over my head."

Kinkaid sighed. "That's right. But we'll find the skunk who shot Sitzman from ambush. Then you'll be clear. Right now you stay close to the house here. I'm already in this as deep as you are. We'll figure something out."

Kinkaid's house was too far from the main street for those inside to hear when the men came back from their fruitless chase of Scott's horse. But they found out soon that the men were back. Scott heard them first — a little slap as someone hit the picket fence in the back yard.

"I think we've got company out there," he said.

"Get away from the windows," Kinkaid said softly. He reached over and blew out the lamp. Immediately sound erupted on all sides of the house.

"You, Kinkaid," a voice shouted. "We've got your place surrounded. Send out that killer."

"That's Russo," Kinkaid said softly. "He may be the one who killed Sitzman."

"That's how I've got it figured," Scott said.

"You hear, Kinkaid?" Russo shouted louder.

"I heard," Kinkaid shouted back. "We don't have any killer in here."

"You've got Scott," Russo said. "Same thing."

"Not in my book," Kinkaid said. "If you want to come in here, get a search warrant."

"We're not fooling with that legal stuff," Russo shouted. "We want Scott. Are you going to send him out? Or do we come in and get him?"

"I'd better go out," Scott said. "There's enough men out there to tear this house apart. If they start shooting, either Anne or Mrs. Kinkaid might get hurt."

"You're not going out there," Anne said quickly. "They'd shoot you the second you stepped through the door."

"Anne's right," Kinkaid said. "Tillotson's offer of five hundred dollars said dead or alive. You can bet they'll make it dead. Especially Russo, if he gets the chance."

"I'm not going to stay here and risk having Anne or Mrs. Kinkaid shot," Scott said positively.

"I don't figure on you staying here," Kinkaid said.

"I'll give you just two more minutes," Russo shouted. "If you haven't sent Scott out here by then, we'll blast you to bits."

"I'm going out," Scott said, moving toward the door.

"You're going out, all right," Kinkaid agreed, "but not that way. Come here." He led the way to the pantry that opened off the kitchen. "See this trap door in the floor?"

Scott nodded. "Where does it go? To the cellar?"

"That's right," Kinkaid said. "There is an outside door to the cellar. But one winter that door was covered

109

with snow most of the time. So I dug an opening here and put in a ladder so we could get into the cellar from the house without scooping all that snow."

"Can I get out of the cellar through the outside door if I go in this way?" Scott asked, getting the picture.

"Yes. We'll keep them busy from here until you have a chance to slip through their lines. Then I'll invite them in to see for themselves that you're not here."

"Hurry, Web," Anne pleaded.

"Don't wait till they start shooting to tell them I'm gone," Scott said as he pulled up the trap door. "I'll make out."

Scott climbed down the ladder, and Kinkaid lowered the trap door over his head. It was pitch dark, but Scott couldn't take time to feel his way along. He heard Kinkaid yell at Russo, asking him if he'd shoot women. Faintly he heard Russo yell back that he'd shoot anybody who stood between him and Sitzman's murderer.

Kinkaid was stalling for time, and it was up to Scott to make good use of every second Kinkaid gained for him. At the bottom of the ladder, Scott turned to his right, where he knew the big door must be. A crack of light seeped into the blackness. It was only a sliver of light, but in the pitch blackness of the cellar, it looked like a beacon.

Scott hit the steps that led up to the door and climbed until his back was pressed against the heavy door. Slowly he lifted. The door began to rise reluctantly, its hinges protesting a little. Scott, with his ears on the level of the hinges, thought the squealing of

110

the hinges must be echoing over the yard like a siren. But there was no sound outside to indicate that the squealing had been heard by anyone else.

Finally the door was lifted enough so that Scott could slip through the opening. He caught the door and let it settle gently back in place. After the pitch blackness of the cellar, the dim light in the yard seemed very bright. Crouching, Scott surveyed the area. Russo had said that he had the house completely surrounded with men. So one direction was as good as another for Scott to try to break through.

In the dim light he crawled slowly across the yard until he reached the picket fence. He remembered that the fence didn't go all the way around the house. Using the pickets as a barrier between him and the men surrounding the house, he moved in a crouching run to the end of the fence.

Peering around the end of the fence, he saw the dim silhouette of a horse standing at the edge of the street. Scott needed a horse, and he knew what he had to do. Moving around the end of the picket fence, he crept toward the horse. He was far enough from the house now so that he knew he must be near the line of men Russo had thrown around Kinkaid's place.

"That time is about gone," Russo shouted, and Scott flattened himself on the ground. Russo was only a few yards to his left.

"He ain't coming out," a man just a few feet from Scott said. "Are you really going to open up with those two women in there?"

"They're harboring a criminal, ain't they?" Russo said. "That makes them just as guilty as the murderer. We'll blast them all if he doesn't come out."

Scott rose to a crouch. If they knew he wasn't in the house they wouldn't start shooting where Anne and Mrs. Kinkaid might be hurt. Besides, he wasn't going to get a horse without letting the men know he was out there.

Running swiftly, he reached the horse before any alarm was given. Then a man only a few feet from the horse yelled and threw himself at Scott. Scott swung the butt of his gun and flattened the man. The next instant he swung into the saddle and wheeled the horse toward open country.

"Get him!" yelled the man Scott had hit as he scrambled to his feet. "That's Scott."

Bullets ripped the night, and Scott heard their snap as they passed him. One burned a path along his ribs, but it was only a scratch. The horse under him sidestepped sharply once, and Scott guessed that the animal had been nicked.

In a few seconds the barrage was over. Scott was out of range of the short guns of the men. He could hear the shouts and the scramble behind as men ran for their horses. It would be only a matter of a minute or two until the men would be mounted and in hot pursuit.

Scott angled toward the creek west of town and raced along its banks. When he heard the noise of the men pounding out of town, he reined his horse to a slower pace and dropped down over the bank into the water willows along the edge of the creek.

Reining up, he leaned forward and put a hand over his horse's nose to prevent a nicker that would tell his pursuers what he had done. Russo's men pounded out of town, racing wildly up the road.

They wouldn't go far, Scott knew, until they would discover that Scott wasn't ahead of them. They'd come back then, looking along the river, the only place where he could have given them the slip.

As soon as the thunder of the hoofbeats had passed, Scott realized that the bullet that had stung the horse back there had gone deeper than he had thought. The horse was limping, favoring his left back leg. The horse wouldn't be much good in a chase. The closest place where he could hope to get a replacement would be the livery barn in town. But his chances of slipping back into town unseen were slight. There couldn't be a sleepy eye in town now, after all that shooting.

In the other direction was the JW. He might find a horse there. Sitzman had fired the crew, and Sitzman himself was dead. Sadie would be the only one on the ranch, unless the cook was still there. And Sadie might have gone somewhere else to spend the night. He certainly wouldn't blame her for not staying there tonight after what had happened. There might be some horses in the corral on the JW. There had been this morning.

Scott reined toward the JW, keeping well south of the creek so Russo's men, if they returned, wouldn't see him. The horse's limp grew progressively worse as Scott urged him toward the JW.

He hit the road leading from the JW to the main road into town. Turning into it, he urged his horse on.

A quarter of a mile from the ranch, the horse's limp became so bad that Scott dismounted. He could lead him the rest of the way. He ran a hand over the horse's hip and felt the spot where the blood was oozing out. The bullet must be in the muscle. Tomorrow in daylight somebody could cut out that bullet, and the horse would be all right. But the horse had done all the running he'd do tonight.

Suddenly Scott heard a distant rumble. He stopped walking, and the horse immediately halted, hanging his head. It took Scott only a second to identify that rumble. Horses.

Evidently Russo's men had discovered that Scott wasn't in front of them on the road west out of town and had doubled back. Scott listened for a minute, getting a line on the direction the horses were going now. What he discovered made him leap into action, jerking on the reins of the horse. The animal resisted the effort to get him to move, and Scott had to tug to get him out of the road.

He led the limping animal toward a swale beyond the knoll to his right. Those horses were coming that way, and they were coming fast.

Scott kept glancing back over his shoulder at the road toward town, expecting to see the bobbing forms of the riders at any moment. Off to his left he could barely see the buildings of the JW, squatting low and dark in the starlight.

He reached the shallow end of the swale and pulled his horse into it. Dragging on the reins, he led the horse along until he had him far enough from the road and deep enough into the low spot so that the men would not see him as they rode past.

The sound of the galloping horses was at Scott's back, and he turned to watch the men ride past. His horse showed no interest in the other horses. Apparently that hip wound had dulled his social instincts.

The horsemen rode into the JW yard and reined up. Even from that distance, Scott heard Russo yell. A light came on in the house, and the front door opened.

After a minute or two, the men began to mill around in the yard. Scott guessed there was a difference of opinion as to where he had gone. Some of the men apparently were ready to give up the chase and go back to town. Scott could hear Russo's voice raised in anger. Obviously Russo wanted to keep looking.

In a few minutes, the men dismounted and went from building to building, searching the entire JW yard and corrals. Scott was thankful he wasn't down there now. Then the men mounted, and most of them rode south. Three turned their horses back to the northeast on the road to town, jogging along slowly.

Scott waited until the men had been gone from the JW for a while and the light went out in the house. Then he started slowly toward the corrals, leading his reluctant horse.

There would be a horse in the corral, Scott was sure. If Sadie was in the house, she couldn't allow herself to be stranded on the ranch without a horse that she could get whenever she wanted it.

Scott led the limping horse into the corral and unsaddled him. There were four horses in the corral next to the one he was in. He hoped he could rope one without causing any commotion. He knew how Sadie felt about him. If she found him taking a horse from the corral, he had no doubt about what she would do.

As he unsaddled the horse, he noticed the brand on his hip: the Tilted T. Sadie wouldn't be too happy in the morning when she found one of Tillotson's horses in her corral.

Scott carried the saddle over to the partition fence between the corrals, took the rope off the saddle horn and crawled in with the four frisky JW horses. Swinging his loop, he made a cast and missed. It was dark and, trying not to stir up the animals, he missed twice more before he managed to get his rope on one of the horses. The horse snorted loudly as he was pulled to the fence where Scott snubbed him and started to saddle him.

"You picked a good one," someone said a few feet away.

Scott, the saddle in his hand, froze. He had no chance to reach for his gun. The fact that it was a woman's voice gave him no comfort. It had to be Sadie. And Scott was sure she would shoot him as quickly as any man would.

"I try to pick the best," he replied.

"Put the saddle down and let's talk a bit," Sadie said.

Slowly Scott turned around until he was facing her. Then he laid the saddle on the ground. "What is there to talk about?"

He expected to see Sadie with a gun in her hand. But she was standing just on the other side of the fence, her arms folded. Now she unfolded her arms and climbed over the fence.

"I figured you'd show up here as soon as Russo was gone," she said. "He told me what happened in town and how you gave them the slip. Russo was sure they had hit either you or your horse. Either way, he didn't figure you'd go too far without help."

"If you had that figured out, why didn't Russo wait for me?"

"I said that I figured it that way, not Russo," Sadie said. "He decided you'd gone on to the south. I didn't tell him what I thought. That was none of his business."

"You wanted me all to yourself. Is that it?"

"Not exactly." Sadie leaned against the fence. "I did a little thinking. You couldn't have killed Pa. He was shot with a rifle, like you said. You didn't have a rifle."

Scott relaxed a little. Maybe Sadie had a decent side to her, after all.

"Are you willing to tell Hookey that?" Scott asked.

Sadie shrugged. "Why not? I want to see the right man hang."

"Why don't we ride into town right now and tell him?" Scott suggested.

"Sounds good to me. Catch another horse and saddle him for me."

Scott finished saddling the horse he had caught. Then he took his rope and went after another horse. He couldn't quell the uneasy feeling he had. This was too sudden a change in Sadie.

He brought the other horse to the corral fence and tied him, putting Sadie's saddle on him.

"I guess we're ready," Scott said, turning to face her.

"I think we are," she said triumphantly, her face beaming in anticipation.

It was then that Scott saw the gun in her hand, pointing straight at his middle.

CHAPTER
ELEVEN

Scott considered making a grab for Sadie's gun before she could fire it. But he knew that he wouldn't stand a chance.

"Changed your mind?" he asked finally.

"Not about riding into town," Sadie said. "We wanted to talk to Sam Hookey. Remember?"

"We won't agree on what to tell him."

"I don't suppose we will," Sadie said, apparently relishing every moment now. "Drop your gun belt."

Carefully Scott obeyed. He didn't doubt for an instant that Sadie would put a hole through him if he showed any inclination to disobey.

"You didn't really think I'd let you have the JW, did you?" Sadie said as she picked up Scott's gun belt. "Pa and I worked hard for this, then Josh double-crossed us by making that will that let you have it. Well, you're not going to get it. With Pa dead, it's all mine. And I'm going to have it."

"Why didn't you shoot me when you first sneaked up on me?" Scott asked, wondering what was going on in her scheming mind. "You could have."

Sadie laughed. "I wanted to see your face when you found out you'd been crossed. Anyway, shooting would have been too easy for you. You've given me nothing but trouble since you came here. You're going to pay for that. You're going to swing, and I'm going to watch it."

"You know I didn't kill your father," Scott said.

"Sure, I know it," Sadie said. "But nobody else knows that I know it. They'll believe what I tell them. And it sure won't be that you're innocent. Now get on your horse. We're going to town."

Scott opened the corral gate and led his horse outside. Sadie stayed behind him all the way, never giving him a chance to make a break. Scott knew that she wouldn't let her desire to see him hang stand in the way of shooting him if he gave her any provocation.

Once on the road away from the ranch, Sadie rode just a few feet to one side and behind Scott, her gun never wavering from him. Scott cursed himself for a fool for having let Sadie get the drop on him.

A half-mile from town, Sadie called a halt. "Sounds like we've got a welcoming committee coming," she said.

Scott nodded. There wasn't enough light to see much. But there were still some lights in town, and the sounds coming toward them were unmistakably made by a group of horses. Scott thought of Russo. But Russo had gone the other way. It wasn't likely that he had gotten back to town yet.

"Going to wait here?" Scott asked. "Those might be my friends."

Sadie snorted. "You haven't got any friends here. You ought to know that by now."

120

Sadie was more nearly right than Scott liked to admit. Since word had gotten around that Scott had shot Sitzman, about the only friends he had left were the Kinkaids.

The horsemen came closer. Then the leader threw a hand in the air, halting them, as he saw Scott and Sadie in the road.

"Who is it?" he shouted, and Scott recognized Hookey's voice.

"Sadie," Sadie yelled back. "And I've got your prisoner, Web Scott."

"Glory be," Hookey said. "That's sure going to save me a powerful lot of riding."

"Let's hang him now," someone behind Hookey shouted. "Save the county the expense of a trial."

"Now hold on," Sadie said. "I brought him in. I've got a little to say about what happens to him. I want to see him dead more than any of you. But I don't want it to be so easy. Let him stew in jail for a few hours; then we'll hang him."

"A few hours is too long for a murderer like him!" the man shouted.

"He goes to jail," another voice said.

Scott turned to stare at the man, not able to see him clearly in the dark. It was J. R. Kinkaid, all right. Scott wondered what he was doing in the posse.

"All right," Hookey said reluctantly. "We'll take him back to jail." He rode close to Sadie. "Don't have much of a posse," he said. "Johnny Russo took most of the best men with him. When Bill came back from the JW and said they hadn't located Scott and that Russo had

121

gone off half-cocked to the south, I knew I had to go after this killer. I picked up what men I could."

"You've got enough," Sadie said. "I took him alone."

When they reached the end of the street, two men surged up to the front of the group, coming in on either side of Hookey.

"I say we ought to string him up right now," one said. "If we wait, something might happen so he could get away."

"No lynching," Kinkaid said sternly. "We've got to have law and order in this country."

"He's right," Hookey said with a show of authority. "It's my duty to see that my prisoner is held for trial."

"Aw, hogwash!" said the man on the other side of Hookey. "I say we should hang him."

But he looked across at Kinkaid as he said it and slowly reined his horse back into the group. Scott knew that it wasn't Hookey who was keeping them from lynching him. It was J. R. Kinkaid. A lot of men in Tomahawk opposed Kinkaid, but they all had respect for him and hesitated to defy him openly.

As they were about halfway through town, the thunder of another group of horsemen came at them from the south. Scott twisted in the saddle to look. He thought he recognized Johnny Russo in the lead. Apparently they had given up their search to the south of the JW and had come back to town.

"We'd better hurry up and get him in jail," Kinkaid said softly to Hookey. "Russo and Kale are both in that bunch. They'll cause trouble."

122

"Sure, sure," Hookey said, apparently undecided what he should do. If he let Russo and Kale take Scott and hang him, it would put Hookey in good with them. But Kinkaid was right there at his elbow, telling him to do his duty.

"Let's get a move on, man," Kinkaid said.

Kinkaid reached over, grabbed the reins of Scott's horse and kicked his own mount into a trot.

"Here, you can't do that," Hookey shouted.

The deputy spurred his horse after Kinkaid. They reached the front of the deputy's office and dismounted just as Russo and Kale yanked their horses to a sliding halt in front of the jail.

"We'll take him right now, Hookey," Russo shouted. "Your job is done."

"Not quite," Kinkaid said. "He's going to jail."

Scott thought of trying to escape. He had no gun, but he wasn't bound. He could run or ride. But he knew he wouldn't be able to get ten feet. Still, even that would be better than hanging. And there was no doubt what Russo would do if he had his way.

"We're taking him," Russo shouted. "Come on, Kale."

Kinkaid suddenly stepped in front of Scott, and he had a gun in his hand. "You'll stay where you belong, Russo. You, too, Kale. Hookey, go in and put Scott in jail."

Russo and Kale stopped, apparently surprised that Kinkaid would take such a strong stand. Hookey, seeing the two gunmen stop, moved quickly to obey Kinkaid's orders. Scott was pushed inside the deputy's office and on to the back, where there were two jail cells. He was shoved into one and the door locked.

He heard Russo arguing outside with Kinkaid, but the doctor wouldn't budge. Finally the voices out front stopped, and feet shuffled away. Kinkaid came into the deputy's office.

"You've got to show a little backbone, Hookey," Kinkaid said. "If you face up to those men, they'll respect you and do what they're told, too."

"Sure," Hookey said importantly. "They won't take my prisoner from me now. I've got him in jail, and he'll stay here until I can get him to the sheriff."

"See that you do that," Kinkaid said. "Russo has gone to get the saloon keeper to open up the saloon. If he does that, you'll have trouble before morning."

"They won't take my prisoner from me," Hookey repeated.

Scott went to the tiny barred window in his cell and looked out. The saloon was right across the side street from the jail. It was dark now, but there were a dozen men standing on the porch.

As he watched, Scott saw Russo come across the street from the hotel, a man at his elbow. The front door of the saloon was opened, and the men swarmed inside. A light soon sprang up inside the saloon, and voices rose in a crescendo. Russo and Kale backed down from Kinkaid's gun a few minutes before, but if they could get some drinks in those men in the saloon, they'd have plenty of help to run over Hookey and drag Scott out of the jail.

Scott looked out to the front office where Hookey sat, toying with his gun. Courage was one thing that Hookey lacked. He hadn't even had enough to come with Russo tonight when he'd tried to get Scott out of Kinkaid's house. Only when prodded later had he taken a posse out to look for Scott. He had probably felt fairly sure then that they would never find him.

When Russo came from the saloon with a following of impatient, half drunk men, Hookey wouldn't stand up to them ten seconds. Scott knew that he was as good as stretching a rope already.

He went back to the window and listened to the shouts and curses over in the saloon. It would take the men a while to work up their courage, but a few bottles of whiskey would take away any hesitancy they might have about hanging a man without a trial.

Scott wondered if Russo wasn't acting on orders. Tillotson wanted Scott out of the way. Probably Russo had orders to get the job done any way that he could. Buying a few bottles of whiskey was a cheap way to get it done.

A stir in the front office took Scott back to the barred door. Anne Kinkaid was in the front office, facing Hookey.

"I want to talk to him," Anne said.

"Nothing doing," Hookey said firmly. "My rule is that nobody sees my prisoner. That includes you and Johnny Russo and anybody else."

"I wish you had nerve enough to enforce that rule," Anne said. "Dad says you'll cave in like a winded pup the minute Johnny Russo or Dan Kale demands that you open up and let them have your prisoner."

Hookey brandished his gun. "I'll stand them off, no matter how many there are or how mean they get. Nobody gets my prisoner."

"It wouldn't hurt to let me talk to him," Anne said.

"Nobody talks to my prisoner," Hookey repeated. "You couldn't have anything to say to him, unless you've got some scheme to help him escape." Hookey's eyes brightened. "Is that it?"

"No," Anne said disgustedly. "My father was the one who insisted he be put in jail."

"That was just to save him from hanging," Hookey said.

Scott knew that Hookey was right about that. But Kinkaid had only delayed the inevitable a short time. As soon as Russo got those men whiskied up, they'd come over. And Hookey would be brushed aside like a straw in a high wind.

"If you let those men take him out of jail and hang him, I'll kill you myself!" Anne said, tears in her voice.

"That's bad, girl," Hookey said. "You're threatening an officer of the law."

"Only if he's too big a coward to do his duty!"

Hookey scowled. "Nobody gets my prisoner," he repeated.

"Better go home, Anne," Scott called to her. "I'll be all right."

"He won't do anything," Anne shouted back.

"You can't, either, Anne," Scott said. "Come back to visit me in the morning."

For a minute, Scott thought Anne was going to refuse to leave. But then she frowned at Hookey and went back outside. Scott returned to the side window and looked across at the saloon. The noise there was increasing as the whiskey began to take effect.

"Hookey, you ought to give me a gun so I can defend myself," he shouted.

Hookey snorted. "That would be smart, wouldn't it? Give a killer a gun and then expect him to sit in jail and wait to be hanged."

"I'm supposed to be waiting for a trial, not a hanging," Scott said.

"Same thing," Hookey said. "Everybody knows you did it."

"Sadie knows I didn't," Scott said.

Hookey came off his chair as if he'd been stung. "How do you know?"

"She told me," Scott said, surprised at the deputy's reaction. "Only she wouldn't tell you or any of the posse. She admitted to me that she knew I didn't kill him, because he was killed with a rifle and I didn't have any."

"You shut up," Hookey said, slumping down at his desk again.

Scott watched the deputy open his desk drawer and take out a bottle. That would be fine! he thought. Hookey, sober, wouldn't be much of a deterrent to Russo and Kale and their men. But Hookey, drunk, would be no good whatsoever.

He went back to the window and watched the saloon. It really didn't make much difference. Drunk or sober, Hookey wouldn't stop Russo and Kale when they came for him. And they would come.

An hour dragged by. Scott heard Hookey grunting and talking to himself out front, and the noise over in the saloon slowly deteriorated into an ominous rumble as Russo and Kale apparently whipped up tempers.

It was sometime after midnight when the front door of the saloon burst open and Dan Kale staggered out. He was followed quickly by Johnny Russo and a dozen other men. Scott decided immediately that neither Kale nor Russo was half so drunk as he was pretending to be.

The men staggered across the street to the deputy's office. Scott turned to see what Hookey was going to do about it. Hookey had left his desk, and he had his gun in his hand as he faced the door.

"That's far enough," he shouted when Kale and Russo burst through the door.

"Now you don't figure on trying to keep us from getting that murderer, do you, Hookey?" Russo demanded.

"He's my legal prisoner," Hookey said. "I can't let anybody have him."

"You ain't letting us have him," Kale said. "We're just plain taking him."

"No, you're not," Hookey said, backing to the iron bars that separated the jail from his office.

"Now just how are you going to stop us?" Russo said, advancing slowly.

"Don't come any closer," Hookey shouted.

128

Russo suddenly whipped out a hand and knocked Hookey's gun aside. "You're too little to be playing with guns. Give me the keys to that bird cage."

Hookey slumped down against the wall to one side of the iron door, and Scott was sure he was crying. But that was of little concern to him now. What did concern him was the haste with which Russo found the keys to the cell and opened the door.

Russo leaped into the cell, and Scott charged into him, slamming him back against the men behind him. Kale, bruised and battered and still limping from the beating Scott had given him earlier that evening, shoved in with two other men. Scott lashed out at them, but more men crowded into the cell until there wasn't room for anyone to fight.

Then somebody pinned Scott's arms to his side, and another man grabbed both his legs. The fight was over.

CHAPTER
TWELVE

Scott continued to struggle as he was dragged from the cell. But he knew it was no use. There were at least a dozen men there, and every one seemed determined to have a hand in hanging him.

Scott had no time to identify any of the men in the mob, other than Johnny Russo and Dan Kale. The others were probably Tilted T hands and the men in town who sympathized with Tillotson, mainly in an effort to win his good favor.

At the door to the deputy's office, they let Scott get to his feet, but two big men held onto each arm.

"Get the rope," Russo shouted.

One of the men ran to the saloon and came back, carrying a coiled rope.

"Let me have it," Russo said. "We'll fix it so he'll lead better."

He took a little time making sure the noose was tied right; then he dropped it over Scott's head. Taking a good grip on the rope, he started off toward the south end of the street.

"Now pull back if you want to die before the official hanging," Russo said.

The others laughed loudly, as though it were a huge joke. Most of the men were drunk, Scott decided. He noticed one man who wasn't laughing and took a good look at him. He was Eli Blessing, the livery stable owner. Scott had been told that he was a Tillotson man. But somehow he didn't seem to be getting much enjoyment out of the hanging.

"See that ridge pole running out from the loft of the barn?" Russo asked when they were almost to the barn. "That's going to take you to the happy hunting grounds, Scott. Look at it good."

"Going to invite Hookey down to see it?" one man asked. "Make it legal, you know."

"He can watch from his office," Kale said. "Safer for him that way."

"Want a horse?" another man asked Russo.

"Don't need it," Russo said. "Eli, bring out a barrel. Let him stand on that."

Eli Blessing nodded and disappeared inside the barn. Scott noticed again that none of the excitement and anticipation that was gripping the other men seemed to possess the livery stable owner. Somewhere along the way he had lost his enthusiasm for the chore.

Scott remembered that Blessing had been the first man he had met in Tomahawk. He had seemed ready enough then to do the will of Cole Tillotson. Scott wasn't questioning the fact that his hanging was Tillotson's will, too. But Blessing no longer seemed so eager to follow it.

One man found a short rope and came up behind Scott, jerking his hands together behind his back and tying them carelessly.

"Hurry it up," Russo shouted through the open door of the barn. "We haven't got all night."

"I don't see why not," Blessing said, coming through the door, rolling a barrel ahead of him.

"I want another drink," Kale said, laughing.

A chorus of shouts greeted Kale's statement. The drinks, Scott thought, were the main thing that held the mob together. And the promise of more free liquor would make them hurry through their grisly business now. Scott doubted if Mark Sitzman had been such a good friend to most of these men that they felt obligated to hang the man they thought had killed him.

Dan Kale helped Blessing set the barrel on end under the ridgepole. Russo lifted Scott up on the barrel, which rocked unsteadily.

"Hold that thing still," Russo snapped to a couple of the men.

Then he stepped back and threw the end of the rope toward the ridge pole. It took three efforts before the rope went over the ridge pole and came back down so Russo could grab it.

"Now then," he said in satisfaction, "any last words, Scott, before I kick this barrel?"

Scott stared at Russo. It hit him suddenly that those were probably his last seconds on earth. Somehow, up till now, it had all seemed fantastic, unreal to him. But with Russo standing there holding the end of the rope and preparing to kick the barrel out from under Scott, it became all too real.

He didn't want to die, not this way. In a battle out in the street, he would feel differently. He'd have his chance. Here he was being killed with no more concern than a man would show for a sheep-killing dog.

Scott realized dimly that these were not the thoughts that a man should have in his last moments of life. He was thinking that Johnny Russo and Cole Tillotson had plagued his life from the time he was just a youngster. They had killed Mike Hammond and laid the blame on Mort Scott, sending him to prison to waste away and die. They had stolen the Crossed S from Scott and saddled him with the stigma of being the son of a jailbird. Now, when he had come for a day of reckoning, they had stamped him with the brand of a killer as they had his father, but this time they were making sure that he died before the truth could come out.

"You know I didn't kill Mark Sitzman," Scott said, glaring at Russo. "Even if I had, it wouldn't make this much difference to you. You wanted him dead more than I did. Why don't you tell them why you're so eager to hang me for killing your worst enemy?"

Russo scowled and drew back his foot to kick the barrel. "Somebody help me hold this rope," he shouted. "I can't do it alone."

One man, not so drunk that Scott's words failed to reach him, pointed a finger at Russo. "Hey, you did hate Sitzman, didn't you?"

Russo turned toward the man, his face brick-red with anger. Then suddenly a new voice rose against him. Eli Blessing stepped up close to Russo where Scott could look directly down on him. He glared at Russo.

"You probably killed Sitzman yourself and are hanging Scott to cover up your tracks!" he shouted.

"That's a lie!" Russo screamed. "Somebody help me hold this rope."

"Just a minute!" Blessing yelled, turning to face the mob. "This is another one of Cole Tillotson's schemes to get rid of an enemy. Scott has been in Tillotson's hair from the day he got to Tomahawk. There is no proof that Scott killed Sitzman. And even if there was, how many of you men loved Sitzman enough to lay yourself open to a prison term to hang his murderer?"

A murmur ran over the men as some of those whose minds weren't completely fogged by Russo's free whiskey began to grasp the situation.

"He's a liar!" Russo screamed, aiming a fist at Blessing.

But Blessing ducked away from the fist, and Russo couldn't follow up without releasing the rope. None of the men had offered to help him hold the rope.

"Prove what you're saying," one man said, leaning toward Blessing.

Blessing nodded. "All right; I will. Tillotson brought me here and gave me the job of running the livery stable. I thought I had a chance to make a decent living. But Tillotson won't allow anybody to do anything decent. I swung a wide loop when I was younger. I got caught and served my time in prison.

134

Tillotson knows that and holds it over me. He'll pull something to send me back to prison if I step out of line. He's told me so in plain words."

"That's what he'll do now, too," Russo shouted.

"Sure, he will if he can," Blessing said. "But I've stood back and kowtowed to him as long as I can. Hanging a man for a murder that I'll bet my soul he didn't commit is too much. It's time we stood up like men and told Cole Tillotson where to head in. He'll hold every one of you responsible for this lynching, and after tonight you'll do what he says or he'll see to it you land in jail. That's how he operates."

Men who had been carried away by the frenzy whipped up by Russo and Kale now suddenly began to sober up and look at their position in the light thrown on it by Eli Blessing. Two or three men in the rear of the mob melted away into the darkness. Several men closer to Russo began nodding their heads in agreement with Blessing.

Then Scott caught another movement out of the corner of his eye. He turned his head. Dan Kale was quietly slipping his gun out of its holster. At that instant Russo, his rage at Blessing getting the better of him, let go of the rope and reached for his gun.

With the end of the rope dangling freely over the ridgepole now, Scott suddenly felt a surge of hope. He had to do something immediately or that hope would be gone. If Russo's or Kale's bullet knocked Blessing out of the picture, the mob would swing back on Russo's side, either voluntarily or from fear.

Kale was too far away for Scott to reach. But Blessing and Russo were right in front of him. Scott launched himself from his barrel, knocking Russo sideways as he reached for Blessing. The rope slithered over the ridgepole, and Scott felt it tighten around his neck. But before it choked off his breath, it whipped over the pole and fell free.

Just as Scott knocked Blessing off his feet, Kale's gun roared. The bullet snapped through the air where Blessing had been a split-second before.

Men yelled and began milling around. Scott couldn't see whether or not anyone tried to disarm Kale. But the hardware owner was out off from the three men on the ground by the milling mob.

Scott rolled free of Blessing, and Blessing lashed out with his gun, slamming it against the side of Russo's head. Then he rolled to his feet, grabbing Scott by the arm.

In the confusion, Blessing pulled Scott into the barn. With one hand, he reached up and flipped the noose over his head.

"Run," he whispered. "They'll be after you the second they realize you're gone."

"They believed you, didn't they?" Scott said. "They don't think I'm guilty."

"I didn't convince them you're not guilty," Blessing said. "I just made them see they were fools to lynch you. They could be sent to prison for that, and Tillotson wouldn't let them forget it."

"So they won't hang me now."

"No," Blessing said impatiently. "But they'll throw you back in that jail. They'll remember that the only two people near Sitzman when he was killed both swear that you did it. Once you're back in that jail, you know what will happen. Tillotson won't try to stir up a mob to kill you next time. He'll find a surer way."

Scott knew that Blessing was right. If he were put back in jail, he'd never walk out again. Somehow he'd be killed right there.

"What about you?" Scott asked.

"I'll take my chances. I risked my life to save yours. Don't stand here and throw it away. Get going!"

Scott turned and ducked into a stall, while Blessing stayed by the door. Scott worked his way quickly to the far end of the barn. But before he could get out, men poured through the front door.

"Where did he go?" one man shouted.

"He slipped away," Blessing said.

"You let him go," another man shouted. "We ought to string you up."

"I just kept you from lynching a man without a trial," Blessing said. "That could keep you out of jail."

Scott still had his hands tied behind his back and tried desperately to work free. He moved around the ink-black stall, searching for something he could use to free himself. Up in the front of the barn, he heard Blessing arguing loudly with the men, insisting that he had done what he had only because he wanted to keep the men from becoming part of a lynch mob.

Scott located a mane roacher in the feed box of the stall. Evidently Blessing used this stall to store some of his tools and gear. He fumbled around until he was holding the mane roacher open, one blade punching around his wrists.

He brought blood a couple of times before he got the scissor-like tool between the ropes holding his wrists. It took only a few strokes across the blade to cut through the ropes, and then his hands were free.

But now the men were running through the barn. Scott crouched in the deep shadows. If they searched the stalls, they'd find him. But they were running through the barn, paying no attention to the stalls. Behind them, Blessing was shouting.

"He must have gone out the back. He came into the barn ahead of me. He wouldn't stop in here."

The men poured through the rear door, and Scott slipped up to the edge of the door and peered outside. There was practically no light in the rear of the barn, but Scott could hear the men running across the street toward the blacksmith shop. Dan Kale had led them through the barn. Perhaps Kale thought that Scott would go back to the blacksmith shop to hide as he had earlier in the evening.

Scott slipped out the back door and pressed himself against the wall of the barn while he listened to the search going on across the street. When the searchers moved on, Scott started back inside. He was sure that Blessing would have a horse or two in the barn. He couldn't remember seeing or hearing any as he ran down the length of the barn. But he hadn't been thinking about horses then. Now he was. He had to have a horse to get out of town. If he stayed around there, somebody would find him. He had no gun; he'd be easy pickings.

If Johnny Russo or Dan Kale found him first, Scott knew he'd be taken in dead. Even if one of the other men found him and took him back to jail, it would amount to practically the same thing. One of Tillotson's men would shoot him through the bars.

As he reached the rear door again, he heard Russo swearing loudly up by the front door. Evidently he had recovered from the clout that Blessing had given him. Scott knew he'd have no chance to slip into the barn and get a horse while Russo was there.

While he was standing there trying to decide what his next move should be, he heard a man out in the street yell to the others:

"Get back in the barn. He may try to get a horse."

Scott heard the thump of boots out in the main street as men ran toward the barn. After listening long enough to be sure that none of the men was coming to the back of the barn, he slipped to the corner and, when the side street was clear, dodged across to the rear of the blacksmith shop.

From there, he ran along the alley to the jail. He remembered that the deputy had left his horse at the hitch rack in front of his office. He had seen it there as the mob was dragging him out of the jail. If he could reach that horse, he might get away before the mob was aware of what he had done.

The saloon was still lighted, but it was empty now. From the rear of the saloon, he looked across the street to the jail. Hookey's horse was still standing in front of

139

his office. No one seemed to be near, so Scott dodged across the street to the rear of the jail. From there, he worked his way to the front of the building on the dark side.

Someone was inside the deputy's office. Scott could hear the voices but he couldn't make out what was being said. He had supposed that Hookey would be out helping hunt the fugitive, now that the danger of his witnessing a lynching was past.

At the window of the deputy's office, Scott stopped and raised his head enough to look inside. Hookey was standing close to the window, a scowl on his face. Scott noted that he didn't appear the least bit drunk now. Standing between him and the door was Sadie Sitzman, and she was as angry as Hookey appeared to be. Their words came clearly to Scott.

"You'll do what I say," Sadie said maliciously, "or you know what will happen to you."

"You can't bluff me with that threat," Hookey said. "Mark tried it, and it got him nowhere."

"It got him killed," Sadie said. "And I know how he was killed, too. You were the only one within a mile of the JW that morning with a rifle. How would the men in town like to know that you killed a man from ambush because he knew that you had murdered a girl years ago?"

"You dare open your mouth about that and I'll — I'll —"

Scott thought that Hookey was going to have a stroke. His face was almost purple, and the veins stood out in his neck and forehead.

"You'll what?" Sadie taunted.

"I'll tell them how you killed Josh Woodruff."

Sadie was visibly rocked by the deputy's accusation. "You can't prove a word of that."

"Can't I?" Hookey said, suddenly gloating as he saw that he had taken the advantage away from Sadie. "A lot of people know how you tried to wangle Josh into marrying you so you could get the JW legally. When he balked at marrying you, you threatened him. I sat right here in my office and saw the whole show that morning. Josh rode in, and you followed him. You rode down to the feed store and waited. Josh was shot from the back of the feed store. Everybody knows that."

"You can't prove a thing."

"I can prove just as much as you can," Hookey said. Suddenly Sadie broke into a laugh. "All right. So I killed Josh. But you won't open your mouth about it. I've got you on two murders. And don't think I won't tell everybody if you so much as get one little step out of line. You're going to do some work for me that only a lawman can do. And you're not going to make one objection."

"I'll object plenty," Hookey said.

Sadie suddenly became furious, her teeth bared in a snarl that reminded Scott of a mad dog. "You do, and I'll turn that mob on you. I guarantee they'll hang you. I'll be there to slap the horse out from under you myself."

Scott, watching, saw panic sweep over Hookey. "You can't push me around!" he shouted.

Sadie suddenly drew her gun and aimed it directly at the deputy. "Who says I can't?"

Scott looked at Hookey. The panic was still there; not even the gun could squelch it. Suddenly Hookey leaped forward. Only a couple of steps separated him from Sadie. His hand struck down, and the gun exploded as it was hit, the bullet plowing into the floor.

Hookey, fighting with a maniac's strength, wrenched the gun from Sadie's hand and stepped back. Quickly and deliberately, he fired twice. Sadie staggered back aganst the wall and slowly slid to the floor.

Shouts and running feet echoed along the street as the men who had been searching for Scott converged on the deputy's office.

Scott watched Hookey throw the gun over close to the front door and run to the door himself and stick his head outside.

"Over here, men!" he yelled. "Scott just shot Sadie Sitzman."

CHAPTER
THIRTEEN

Scott froze in his crouch below the window. Hookey couldn't possibly know that Scott was close by. But he had certainly heard that he had escaped the lynching party and that the men were searching for him. So it had apparently struck him that he might be able to blame Sadie's murder on Scott.

But the fact that Scott was right there by the deputy's office now put Scott in the worst possible position. When the men arrived at the jail, they'd begin searching there, believing that Scott was close by. If Scott was found there, there would be no doubt as to his guilt in anybody's mind.

The urgency of getting away drove Scott into action. He turned and ran to the rear of the jail. Out front, he heard a man yell at Hookey as he came running toward him.

"Why did he shoot Sadie?"

As he ran along the rear of the jail, Scott heard Hookey's reply.

"She was the only one who actually saw him kill Mark Sitzman. I guess he figured if she was dead, nobody could prove he did it."

"Why did he kill her right in your office?"

"He tried to kill us both," Hookey said. "With both of us gone, there would have been no proof at all."

Scott heard no more. Glancing up the side street, he saw that it was empty for the moment, and he dashed across to the rear of the saloon, then he ran full speed down the alley behind the buildings. Reaching the back of the blacksmith shop, he paused to make sure the side street between the shop and the livery stable was empty.

Just as he was ready to dash across the dusty street, a rider burst out of the rear door of the barn and angled into the street only a few feet from Scott. Putting the spurs to his horse, he kicked up a fog as he charged out of town to the east.

Shouts up from the main street, and feet pounded down the boardwalk and along the dusty street again.

"He got a horse at the barn," some man yelled. "Let's catch him."

"Hold on!" another man shouted. "That couldn't be Scott. He hasn't had time to get a horse."

Scott was sure that was Cole Tillotson's voice. He hadn't known that Tillotson was in town. Apparently he had come in after Scott had been thrown in jail. Probably he had come to witness the hanging, although he had been careful not to get in the mob itself.

"He's getting away," another man yelled. "Let's get him."

Scott crouched low in the shadows at the rear of the blacksmith shop, while men ran to the livery stable and the hitch rack in front of it where some of them had their horses.

144

"You idiots!" shouted another voice that Scott identified as belonging to Johnny Russo. "That wasn't Scott. If he shot Sadie, he couldn't have gotten to the barn yet."

But the men were convinced that Scott had somehow gotten to the barn and taken a horse and was now riding out to the east, getting away from them.

Suddenly the whole street seemed to explode with thundering hoofs as the men reached their horses and mounted. Scott remained low in the shadows as they raced by, although he was sure they wouldn't have seen him if he'd stood right at the side of the street. They had only one purpose in mind — to catch the rider who had rushed out of town ahead of them.

When the riders were gone, Scott scanned the side street again. There was no sign of movement there, and he dashed across it to the rear of the livery stable. Going in the back door, he stopped in the shadows.

Up toward the front of the building, a lantern swung from a snap that slid along a wire running the length of the barn. From that snap, the lantern could be slid along until it shed light in any given stall. Standing close to the lantern was Eli Blessing.

Scott tried to see into the stalls along the length of the barn. Surely there would be at least one horse left. But he couldn't see any. If he could get a horse and ride to the west or south, his chances of getting out of the country would be good. Some day he'd come back and prove his innocence, but right now his only chance, the way he saw it, was to get out of Tomahawk Valley.

He moved along the stalls far enough to see that there were no horses in the barn. There were horses in the corral to the south of the barn, he knew. But he didn't dare go after one. Maybe Blessing would get one for him. He had helped Scott already tonight. He might help him some more.

Halfway along the row of stalls, Scott called a low warning to Blessing. The stable owner looked at him without any show of surprise.

"Can you get me a horse?" Scott whispered.

Blessing moved toward him. "I think so," he said softly.

Scott stepped back into the dark stall and waited for Blessing to come to him.

"We've still got company outside," Blessing said softly when he reached Scott. "Cole Tillotson is out there. And Russo and Kale didn't ride off with the other men. They figured out it wasn't you."

"Who was it?" Scott asked.

"It was George Ingram. He'd been trying to persuade the lawyer, Edris, to help him get rid of you and give him legal title to the JW. Edris couldn't do that, of course, but Ingram wouldn't believe it. From what I gathered from Ingram when he was in here getting a horse, he and Edris had a fight. Ingram hit the lawyer over the head with some kind of iron bar, and he thinks he killed him. So he's running away. Never saw anybody more scared than that fellow."

"How about getting a horse for me?" Scott asked.

"I'll do it pretty soon. You don't want to tear out of here until that posse gets well out of town. The rate

146

Ingram was going, it will take those men at least a couple of hours to catch him. He had a good horse. Besides, if I rush out into the corral to get a horse, you can bet Tillotson or one of his two gunmen will figure out why I'm doing it."

"All right," Scott said reluctantly. "But I don't feel comfortable sitting around here. Tillotson and Russo and Kale must be pretty certain I'm still in town."

"Reckon they are," Blessing said. "But they don't have any idea where you are. If I went out to catch a horse, they'd know."

"Tillotson can just about claim this whole valley now," Scott said, "with both the Sitzmans dead."

"You're not," Blessing said. "That's the one thorn left in Tillotson's side. He owns practically everybody in this town. I told them out there what he's holding over me. Not much, maybe, but enough to make me toe the mark. At least it was until tonight. I just figured I couldn't ever live with myself if I let them lynch you, knowing that Russo probably killed Sitzman."

"Hookey did it," Scott said. "I heard Sadie accuse him of it. Seems Sitzman knew that Hookey had killed a girl back east somewhere and was blackmailing him. I didn't suspect Hookey; I had no idea he had any reason to kill Sitzman."

Blessing whistled softly. "That proves how wrong a man can be if he doesn't know all the facts. Probably the murder of that girl is the thing Tillotson holds over Hookey, too. I know he owns him, body and soul. Russo and Kale are just plain mean, the kind of killers men like Tillotson have to have around them to keep everybody else in line. I figure Tillotson pays them plenty. I hear that Russo and Kale were in prison together."

"Ought to be there now," Scott added. "What will happen to you now that you've kicked over the traces?"

Blessing was silent for a moment. "I reckon I'll have to face either Johnny Russo or Dan Kale, probably before another day is over."

"Why did you do it, when you knew what would happen?"

"I got fed up," Blessing said emphatically. "I'm filled up to here with kowtowing to Cole Tillotson."

"Maybe you'd better get two horses from the corral," Scott said. "Looks to me like we'd better both ride out of here."

"I'm not much on running," Blessing said. "I've done a lot of it in my time, and each time I did, I got a little sicker of it. When I took this job at Tillotson's request, I made up my mind I'd run an honest barn. When it got to the point where I couldn't do that, I'd make my stand. I reckon I've reached that point."

Silence fell between them. Scott wondered how long it would be before Blessing thought it would be safe to go out and bring a horse in from the corral. And he wondered, too, if Tillotson would let him get a horse. He didn't doubt now that Blessing was on Tillotson's list of men to be eliminated, the same as Scott was.

Scott thought he heard a sound at the rear of the barn and turned that way. Neither he nor Blessing made any noise. Scott was sure that Blessing had heard it, too. Maybe Tillotson or one of the men had decided to have a look inside the barn.

The light thrown by the lantern was almost completely absorbed by the darkness back at the rear of the barn, and it was nearly pitch black in the stall where Scott and Blessing were. Scott could see the square opening of the rear door which showed a block of dark blue sky studded wtih stars. There was nothing blotting out those stars at the moment.

Then Scott heard the sound again and wheeled as he realized he'd been looking in the wrong place. In that instant, a voice cut through the stillness. "Don't move, Scott. I've got my gun right in the middle of your backbone."

Scott saw the man then. In the darkness of the stall, he was just a dim outline. He was standing behind Blessing and apparently had mistaken Blessing for Scott. Scott recognized Hookey's voice. The deputy was the last man in town that Scott would have expected to sneak in to try to take him single-handed. Apparently Hookey hadn't seen Scott yet.

Scott moved forward silently. When he struck, he'd have to do it quickly, unerringly. Hookey played into Scott's hands then by stepping back a little from Blessing.

"Let's go outside, Scott," the deputy said. "Walk straight and easy toward that front door."

Blessing moved a step ahead, and in that instant, Scott struck. His hand came down like the edge of an iron bar across Hookey's wrist, sending his gun into the litter at his feet. His other arm came up, encircling the deputy's neck.

"Get his gun," Scott said.

Blessing had already turned. "Got it," he said a moment later. "Now what will we do with him?"

"Wish we could get him all alone at a time like this," Scott said.

"We won't catch any of the others this easy," Blessing said. "They're not as thick-headed as this one. He thought he had you. But what did he think I'd be doing all the time he was marching you out of here? He surely knew I was here in the barn, too."

"Let's make him do some talking and find out," Scott suggested.

He took Hookey's gun from Blessing and shoved it into the deputy's back, releasing his hold on his throat. "Got anything to say, Hookey?"

The deputy just stood there, saying nothing. Blessing prodded him from the other side, but still Hookey remained silent.

"Let's take him to one of the stalls where the lantern throws a little more light," Blessing said. "I figure Tillotson has some scheme afoot, and this jasper may know what it is. Maybe we can make him talk."

"I won't talk," Hookey said.

Scott prodded him up to one of the stalls toward the front of the barn where the light was stronger.

"You make quite a habit of killing people when they can't fight back, don't you?" Scott said.

"I don't know what you're talking about," Hookey said sullenly.

150

"First there was that woman years ago," Scott said. "Then Mark Sitzman this morning. Tonight, it was Sadie Sitzman."

"They think you killed Sadie," Hookey said, a note of triumph in his voice.

"You and I know different. You are nearer right than you thought on one point, though. I was close to your office when Sadie was shot. I saw you shoot her."

"That's a lie!" Hookey said sharply. "Nobody saw —"

"Oh, yes, I did," Scott interrupted. "I was looking through that little window in the north side of your office. You jerked the gun away from her and deliberately shot her twice."

Realization of the truth began to seep into the deputy's face. And with it came a fear that bordered on panic.

"You might as well admit it," Blessing said. "You know that Scott is telling the truth. He saw you do it."

"All right," Hookey said. "So I killed her. She'd have killed me if I hadn't."

"Tell that to the men out there."

"They'll string you up for shooting a woman," Blessing said, "even if it is a woman they wanted out of the way. They probably would like to find an excuse to get rid of you, anyway. You know how much Tillotson loves you."

"Shut up!" Hookey shouted. "Tillotson wouldn't hurt me. I've always helped him."

"That's not the way I hear it from Cole," Blessing said.

151

In the dim light from the lantern, Scott could see the sweat breaking out on Hookey's forehead. The deputy obviously was deathly afraid of Cole Tillotson.

"I've done whatever Tillotson asked me to do," Hookey said.

"Like killing Sadie?" Scott asked.

"He wanted her dead, anyway," Hookey said. "He's going to own this whole valley before the week is out. I heard him say so myself."

"What's he planning to do right now?" Blessing asked.

"He's got it all figured," Hookey said. "He —"

A shot ripped through the barn. Scott and Blessing dived back deeper into the stall Hookey dropped flat.

"I'm hit! I'm hit!" the deputy screamed.

Scott reached out and dragged Hookey deeper into the stall. The shot, he was sure, had come from the back door. Where Hookey had been sitting, he had been partially exposed to the door. Deeper in the stall, he was not.

"Let's see how bad you're hurt," Scott said.

The light from the lantern was weak that far back, but it was strong enough to show a bloody scratch across the upper arm of the deputy.

"Just a scratch," Blessing said disgustedly. "Not a deep one, either. The way you yelled, I thought you were half dead."

"They're trying to kill me," Hookey blubbered. "They're trying to kill me."

"Why, Tillotson wouldn't do that," Scott mocked.

"You help him all the time, you said."

152

"He tried to kill me," Hookey repeated as if dazed by the fact.

More shots ripped into the barn. Hunching down deep in the stall, the three were safe from the probing bullets. But Scott wasn't satisfied to stay there.

"They can't hit us," he said to Blessing, "but we can't shoot back, either. They might sneak inside the barn if we aren't out where we can watch."

"You're right," Blessing said. "We've got to get out of this trap."

Scott crouched, gun in his hand, as he surveyed the situation. From a stall in the center of the barn, he would be fairly well protected from either door while able to keep those doors under surveillance.

"Coming?" he said to Blessing as he prepared to make a dash.

"Right behind you," Blessing said. "Come on, Hookey."

Scott suddenly darted out of the stall and dodged around the end of the stalls till he reached the one he wanted. Guns opened up from both doors, but no bullets hit him.

Once in his stall, Scott began shooting first at one door, then at the other. Under cover of Scott's firing, Blessing made the dash to the stall without trouble.

"Now what?" Blessing asked after he caught his breath. "We're in a fairly safe spot. But we still can't do much damage to them."

"It will be just a lucky shot if either of us hits anything. Looks to me like a stand-off."

"It will be unless they decide to smoke us out," Blessing said.

Scott nodded. That was the big advantage that Tillotson and his men held now. One match in the dry hay, and the livery barn would go up like a tinderbox.

CHAPTER
FOURTEEN

The shooting continued spasmodically for an hour. Scott noticed after a time that there was no longer any shooting from the rear door. He called Blessing's attention to that.

"Could be a trap," Blessing said. "Maybe they think we'll try to make a run for it through that back door. They'd be waiting for us."

Scott nodded. "Could be. Where's Hookey?"

"I've been wondering about that. I told him to follow me. Maybe he's still crouching back there under the manger in the front of that stall. He'd be safe there, you know."

Scott nodded. "Maybe. One thing sure: he won't take a hand in the shooting if he can help it."

"Only two things can make Hookey fight," Blessing said. "One is to give him an advantage so he runs no risk of geting hurt, the way it was when he killed Mark Sitzman. The other is to corner him. Any rat will fight when he's cornered."

"Like he did when Sadie threw her gun on him?"

"I reckon," Blessing said. "Once he got the advantage, he killed her without turning a hair. He's not the kind of man I'd want to call a friend."

Scott agreed with Blessing on that. "What do you figure Tillotson will do now?"

"Hard to say," Blessing returned. "It will be daylight soon. The men who rode out after Ingram should figure out their mistake when they see him, if they don't catch him or lose his trail before then."

"Do you think Tillotson will just sit tight till they get back? Or will he burn us out?"

"I doubt if he'll do that if he can find any other way," Blessing said. "He owns this barn, you know. I just worked for him. He won't destroy any of his own property if he can help it."

Scott decided that Tillotson would probably wait until the men returned. Then he'd have a force strong enough to run roughshod over Blessing and Scott. An occasional bullet slapped into the heavy wood of the stall, more of a reminder that they were not forgotten, Scott thought, than an attempt to inflict any damage.

Once, during the darkest hour just before dawn, Scott heard a yell at the front of the barn. It was a weird, panic-stricken yell and defied any attempt to identify the man who gave it. It was followed a couple of minutes later by two shots. But no bullets slammed into the barn.

"Something funny is going on out there," Blessing said.

"Maybe they're fighting among themselves," Scott suggested.

"That would be too good to be true," Blessing said. "But I sure can't figure out that yell and those shots."

After that dark hour, the eastern sky began to lighten. The gray fingers of dawn crept slowly through the rear door of the barn and stretched across the littered floor.

The lantern, which had given what light there had been inside the barn through the night, seemed to fade until the yellow flame behind the round globe was only a tiny slice of color lost in a brightening world.

"I don't want to spend the day here," Scott said. "I'm going to try to get out the back door while it is still pretty dark."

"Be careful," Blessing warned. "They may be waiting for us to try that very thing."

"I can see well enough now to get a good look out there."

"I'll stay here and put up a cover for you," Blessing said.

Scott clutched his gun in one hand, picked his course before leaving the protection of the stall, then dived into the alley of the barn. A bullet dug up litter behind him as a surprised gunman at the front door snapped a shot at him. Blessing opened up from the safety of the stall, driving back the man at the front door.

Scott reached the back door and stopped, peering around the corner. The light wasn't very strong out there, but it was strong enough to assure Scott that nobody was in sight.

Dodging outside, he paused, his gun ready. In spite of the fact that he knew someone might be waiting in ambush, he felt safer there than he had at the door,

157

knowing the man at the far end of the barn might brave Blessing's marksmanship to get a shot at Scott's back.

There was no sound in the alley, and Scott ran to the corner of the barn. The man at the front of the barn knew that Scott had gone out the back way. Someone would be around to get him. They couldn't let him get away from the barn where he could become the hunter instead of the hunted.

There was no one in the side street between the barn and the blacksmith shop, and Scott ran along the side of the barn. He was halfway to the front when a man charged around the corner in front of him.

Both Scott and the man stopped as though they had hit an invisible wall. Johnny Russo stood there in front of Scott, his gun in his hand.

Scott brought up his gun at the same instant that Russo did his. The two shots blended into one. But Scott was already falling as he shot, a trick that Cole Tillotson had taught him during the days when Scott's father had objected to Scott learning so much about handling a gun.

Scott's bullet went straight into Russo's chest, while Russo's bullet merely tugged at the sleeve of Scott's shirt as it snapped past. There were no more shots from either gun. Russo staggered a step forward and sprawled in the dust, while Scott waited, his gun ready.

Scott got to his feet and walked forward carefully. He had to be sure the danger frrom Johnny Russo was past. Even if it was, there was still danger from the other guns. Dan Kale and Tillotson were somewhere in town. And he had no idea where Sam Hookey was.

Scott approached the spot where Russo had fallen and saw from the way Russo was crumpled in the dust that he had no more to fear from him. As he looked down at Russo, something slammed into the side of the barn only inches from Scott's head. Instinctively Scott dropped to the ground as the report of a rifle echoed along the street.

Rolling over once, Scott took a quick look up the street. Not much of it was visible to him from there. The corner of the blacksmith shop shut off much of his view of the main street. He could see the feed store and barbershop across the street and one corner of the hardware store. There was a little puff of smoke coming from the doorway of the hardware store.

Scott rolled toward the blacksmith shop as two more bullets dug into the dirt in his wake. Then he was out of sight of the hardware store and got to his feet. The man at the hardware must be either Kale or Tillotson. Scott had to get closer or he'd be no match for a man with a six-gun. Not only that, but whoever was in the store had the building for protection. Scott had nothing.

Scott thought of dodging across the street, taking his chances on moving fast enough so that the man couldn't hit him. From over there he could come up on a side of the hardware building that had no windows. But he discarded that plan. Somewhere in town was at least one more man waiting for him. Chances were he was in front of the livery barn. If Scott dodged into the street, trying to escape the bullets of the man in the hardware, he'd be easy picking for the other man.

Dodging around behind the blacksmith shop, he ran along the alley. He stopped to catch his breath behind the harness shop, directly across from the hardware. But still there was a street between him and the store, and Scott knew he could never get across it from there.

There had been no sound from the rifleman in the hardware store since he had shot at Scott down by the barn and Scott began to wonder if the man might have decided to abandon his position. If he did, all of Scott's maneuvering would be wasted. Even worse, the man might move to a place where he could get a clear shot at Scott.

All Scott could do was hope the man stayed in his protected position in the store. It would be hard to rout him out, but that would be safer for Scott than having to hunt for him.

Scott ran on up the alley, crossing behind the dry goods store and the saloon. In the street between the saloon and the deputy's office, he turned toward the main street. At the corner of the saloon, he paused to scan the front of the hardware store. The rifle was still there at the open door, although Scott couldn't see the man behind it.

The light wasn't strong yet. That had probably saved his life back there by the livery barn. But, close as he was to the store now, it wouldn't save him again. From the angle of the rifle barrel, Scott guessed that the man still thought he was down by the barn. That would give Scott an extra second in his dash across the street. And he had to cross the street before he could hope to meet the rifleman on anything resembling even terms.

160

Drawing a deep breath, Scott launched himself into a zigzag run across the street toward the hotel. He was more than halfway across before the rifle opened up. But the man had been in too big a hurry to switch directions with the rifle, and the bullet struck five feet behind Scott. Scott threw himself in a headlong dive behind the north end of the hotel veranda. The rifle roared again, but the bullet hit the veranda, and Scott breathed a relieved sigh.

Getting to his feet, he ran along the side of the hotel and around the back. The hardware was next to the hotel, with a wide alley between. Dr. Kinkaid's office in the corner of the hotel opened into the alley.

There was no window in the north side of the hardware store, and Scott didn't hesitate a second as he came to the alley. The man in the store would be hurrying toward the back door now, knowing that Scott planned to come that way. Scott had to beat him to it.

As he ran across the alley, Scott noted that there was a light in the Kinkaid house to the west. A light wasn't needed outside now but inside a house it would be. Apparently Dr. Kinkaid was up; maybe his whole family. With so much shooting going on, it would be odd if everyone in town wasn't awake and watching.

Reaching the rear of the hardware store, Scott paused. The rifleman had had time to get to the back door. But everything was quiet there. Scott wondered if the door was locked. Moving cautiously to it, he stood to one side and tried the knob. The door slowly swung open.

Scott knew that the man must be waiting to blast him the instant he appeared in that doorway. Still, he had to get inside.

Scott found a small box at his feet and picked it up. He tossed it through the doorway, and the rifle roared. The box was splintered in mid-flight. The instant the rifle fired, Scott dived through the door, hitting the floor and rolling. The rifle roared again, but the bullet was off target.

Scott came to his knees, his eyes on the spot where he had seen the flash of the rifle in the deep gloom inside the store. Scott fired twice. Then he dived behind some cases that were stacked at one side of the door.

The rifle fired again, then was quiet. The next bullet that slammed into the cases came from a hand gun. Scott found some satisfaction in the realization that the fight was on even terms at last.

He dodged to another pile of boxes, getting a better view of the place where the man was hidden. He was in the main part of the store, crouched behind a counter. On the counter almost directly above the man's head was a glass-bowled lamp half full of kerosene. Apparently the man had had it lit; then the shooting down at the barn when Scott had met Russo had drawn his attention. He had taken a hand in the fight and had blown out the lamp to keep the interior of the store dark.

Scott fired again, this time aiming at the big bowl of the lamp. Glass shattered and kerosene splashed over everything close to it. The man behind the counter suddenly leaped up, howling, as glass and kerosene showered over him.

Scott moved out from behind the boxes, gun in hand, as Dan Kale came over the counter, rubbing his eyes.

"Stop right there, Kale," Scott ordered. "Drop that gun."

The gun clattered to the floor. "I can't see!" Kale howled.

"That's fine," Scott said. "What were you doing here instead of being down at the barn?"

"I came after more shells for my rifle," Kale said sullenly.

Scott nodded. "Were you guarding the back door of the barn?"

"For a while," Kale said. "Let me wash this kerosene out of my eyes."

"Where's Hookey?" Scott demanded. "Have you seen him?"

Kale swore. "Get me some water."

Scott directed Kale to a water bucket he had spotted on a stool by another counter. Kale plunged his hands and face into the bucket, rubbing his eyes.

"Have you seen Hookey?" Scott repeated.

"Yes," Kale said. "He sneaked out of the barn a while after we started shooting. We let him come out, and he swore he was going to kill Tillotson before Cole killed him. Tried it, too. Got on top of the barn and tried to drop that rope around Cole's neck; the one Russo planned to hang you with."

"I suppose Hookey missed," Scott said. "He never did anything right in his life."

"He did worse than miss," Kale said, rubbing his face with a rag he found by the bucket. "He got tangled up in that rope somehow and hung himself by the foot. He's still hanging from that ridgepole, head down."

"Alive?"

"No. Johnny shot him. Tillotson's orders."

The back door opened cautiously, and Kinkaid stuck his head inside.

"All clear in here?" he asked.

"All quiet," Scott said. "Come on in. Can you lock Kale up in the jail? Seems we don't have a deputy any longer."

"Be glad to," Kinkaid said, moving quickly inside the store. "I've been doctoring Berwyn Edris. He got a nasty crack on the head, but he'll be all right."

Anne came in the back door. "Are you all right, Web?" she asked.

"Sure," Scott said. "But you'd better get back home. This isn't over yet."

"Why not? It —"

Her words were cut off by a burst of gunfire coming from the livery barn. Scott ran to the front of the store and out on the porch. He stopped there, trying to see what was happening. The sun wasn't yet up, but the dusk in the street was rapidly melting away.

Eli Blessing stumbled out the door of the barn as another shot echoed along the street from the direction of the feed store. Blessing jerked around and went down. But immediately he began to crawl toward the corner of the barn.

Scott ran into the street, firing at the feed store to draw the attention of the man there. It had to be Tillotson. The men who had ridden out after Ingram were not back yet. All the others who had remained in town were accounted for.

Tillotson turned his gun on Scott, and Scott dived back into the protection of the alley between the hardware store and the barbershop. The feed store was just beyond the barbershop.

"Come on out, Cole," Scott yelled. "Russo's dead and Kale's headed for jail. You're finished."

"Come and get me!" Tillotson yelled back.

Scott looked across the street. If he were over there, he might be able to blast Tillotson out of the feed store. But Tillotson would pick him off if he tried to dodge across. He might come in the back door of the feed store as he had come in on Dan Kale. But facing Kale's gun was one thing; facing Cole Tillotson's was another.

Still, going in the back door was the only way, and Scott knew it. He moved along the side of the barbershop to the rear corner and stepped around it. Just as he did, the rear door of the feed store burst open and Tillotson leaped out, firing as he came. He evidently had been waiting for Scott to make that very move. Having taught Scott how to fight that kind of battle, he knew what to expect from him.

Although Scott was caught by surprise, his reaction was instantaneous. He threw himself sideways, bringing his gun to bear as he went down. Tillotson's bullet dug

165

into Scott's arm, while Scott's bullet missed its target completely.

Scott rolled twice. When he stopped, he saw the Tilted T owner steadying himself on one knee to make sure of his aim. Scott threw himself sideways again, firing as he did so. Tillotson's shot missed completely this time, but Scott's bullet knocked Tillotson backward.

Tillotson rolled over, bringing his gun up hastily. Scott fired again, his bullet driving into Tillotson's shoulder. Tillotson dropped his gun and flopped back on the ground. But he was up in an instant, reaching for the gun with his left hand.

Scott was on his feet then, running toward Tillotson. "Don't do it, Cole!" he shouted. "I'll kill you."

"Why not?" Tillotson hesitated only for a moment to glare up at Scott. "Go ahead and shoot."

Just as Tillotson's left hand closed on the gun, Scott put a foot on his wrist.

"Drop it!"

Only after Scott put heavy pressure on the wrist did Tillotson let his fingers relax. The gun dropped back to the ground.

"Why couldn't you kill me and be done with it?" Tillotson asked, pinching his lips together against his pain.

"That would be too easy," Scott said. "You've got a lot to pay for. Come on. The doc can fix you up."

Kinkaid was just opening his office after taking Kale to the jail and motioned for Scott to bring his prisoner there. While Kinkaid worked on Tillotson, Scott went back to the barn and got Eli Blessing. Blessing wasn't hurt as badly as Scott had feared and was able to walk to the doctor's office without help.

"What are you going to do with me now?" Tillotson demanded weakly when Scott got back to the office.

"I'm going to give you a choice, Cole. When those men get back from chasing Ingram, they're going to be plenty sore, but sober. They'll be ready to listen to the truth. You can clear the Scott name of the murder for which Mort was convicted, or I'll tell those men exactly how you've been using them and let them pass judgment on you."

Tillotson paled. "They'd hang me," he croaked.

"If they decide that's what you deserve, why not?" Scott said.

Tillotson debated only for a minute, then nodded. "All right," he said wearily. "I'll tell the authorities what really happened. It was Johnny Russo who killed Hammond; not Mort Scott. We framed Mort so I could get the Crossed S. I figured at first that I'd take you along with me, almost as my son. That's why I taught you how to handle a gun so well. But you were too stubborn; you had to go on your own. Together we could have owned a half-dozen counties, Web, and controlled everything in this end of the state, from cattle to politics."

"What about that ten thousand dollars you stole from me?" Scott asked as if he hadn't heard what Tillotson had said.

Tillotson sighed. "I'll sign over the Tilted T. That will pay you back with interest. I'll have no more use for it."

"I'll put Tillotson in jail with Kale," Kinkaid said. "Then I'll fix up you and Eli. You'll have to ride to the county seat and bring the sheriff. I don't want the responsibility of these prisoners any longer than necessary."

Scott nodded. He wasn't surprised that Kinkaid could take over authority so easily. He had been the one pillar of strength opposing Tillotson.

Kinkaid finished bandaging Tillotson, then guided him across the street to the jail. Scott turned to see Anne staring steadily at him.

"Now you'll own the whole valley," Anne said. "You already own the JW."

Scott sensed her resentment. "The JW belongs to your father," he said. "He owns the mortgage. As for the Tilted T, most of the land controlled by Tillotson doesn't belong to the ranch at all. Homesteaders will soon file on that. I won't have a very big ranch; maybe not big enough for a doctor's daughter."

Anne flushed. "A soddy on a homestead will be big enough for me," she said, all her resentment gone, "providing I have the right man with me."

"And who is that going to be?" he asked.

"You guess," she said softly, ignoring Eli Blessing lying on the couch as she came to Scott's arms.

She left no room for guessing. And that was the way Scott liked it.

Wayne C. Lee was born to pioneering homesteaders near Lamar, Nebraska. His parents were old when he was born and it was an unwritten law since the days of the frontier that it was expected that the youngest child would care for the parents in old age. Having grown up reading novels by Zane Grey and William MacLeod Raine, Lee wanted to write Western stories himself. His best teachers were his parents. They might not be able to remember what happened last week by the time Lee had reached his majority, but they shared with him their very clear memories of the pioneer days. In fact they talked so much about that period that it sometimes seemed to Lee he had lived through it himself. Lee wrote a short story and let his mother read it. She encouraged him to submit it to a magazine and said she would pay the postage. It was accepted and appeared as *Death Waits at Paradise Pass* in *Lariat Story Magazine*. In the many Western novels that he has written since, violence has never been his primary focus, no matter what title a publisher might give one of his stories, but rather the interrelationships between the characters and within their communities. These are the dominant characteristics in all of Lee's Western fiction and create the ambiance so memorable in such diverse narratives as *The Gun Tamer* (1963), *Petticoat Wagon Train* (1972), and *Arikaree War Cry* (1992). In the truest sense Wayne C. Lee's Western fiction is an outgrowth of his impulse to create imaginary social fabrics on the frontier and his stories are intended primarily to entertain a reader at the same time as to articulate what it was about these pioneering men and women that makes them so unique and intriguing to later generations. His pacing, graceful style, natural sense of humor, and the genuine liking he feels toward the majority of his characters, combined with a commitment to the reality and power of romance between men and women as a decisive factor in making it possible for them to have a better life together than they could ever hope to have apart, are what most distinguish his contributions to the Western story. His latest novel is *Edge of Nowhere* (1996).

ISIS publish a wide range of books in large print, from fiction to biography. Any suggestions for books you would like to see in large print or audio are always welcome. Please send to the Editorial Department at:

ISIS Publishing Limited
7 Centremead
Osney Mead
Oxford OX2 0ES

A full list of titles is available free of charge from:

Ulverscroft Large Print Books Limited

(UK)
The Green
Bradgate Road, Anstey
Leicester LE7 7FU
Tel: (0116) 236 4325

(Australia)
P.O. Box 314
St Leonards
NSW 1590
Tel: (02) 9436 2622

(USA)
P.O. Box 1230
West Seneca
N.Y. 14224-1230
Tel: (716) 674 4270

(Canada)
P.O. Box 80038
Burlington
Ontario L7L 6B1
Tel: (905) 637 8734

(New Zealand)
P.O. Box 456
Feilding
Tel: (06) 323 6828

Details of **ISIS** complete and unabridged audio books are also available from these offices. Alternatively, contact your local library for details of their collection of **ISIS** large print and unabridged audio books.